Heart

Short stories from the 2023 inaugural
Mansfield Readers and Writers Festival

Mansfield
Readers &
Writers
storytelling in all its forms

Published by Mansfield Readers & Writers Incorporated in 2023

www.mansfieldreadersandwriters.com

ISBN: 978-0-6457242-0-2 (ebook)
ISBN: 978-0-6457242-1-9 (paperback)

A catalogue record for this book is available from the National Library of Australia

Contents

Introduction

When we decided to include a short story competition in our inaugural festival we had no idea how far it would reach. For us, as a committee of dedicated readers and writers this was simply a way to signal our commitment to reading and writing, to set the ball rolling and stick our heads above the parapet. And then the entries started rolling in; from our local area and from all around Australia. In fact every State and Territory was represented among the more than 100 entries received, each responding to the competition's theme of 'heart'.

And what responses they were!

The long listing process left us with 40 stories and within that, a short list of 5 very different tales, each compelling in its own way. As a committee, we've all read all of the stories in this anthology. We laughed, we cried and we are proud to present them to you as part of the inaugural Mansfield Readers and Writers Festival.

We would like to thank Laurie Steed, our steadfast judge and an expert in the short story form. Thank you for reading our incredibly long,

long list and providing thoughtful feedback and expert guidance.

We thank all the writers who entered a story in the competition. The celebration of storytelling is at the heart of what we're trying to achieve at Mansfield Readers and Writers, and as storytellers you are doing important work.

And our heartfelt thanks to you, the reader. Writers need readers, as much as readers need writers. We commend these stories to you and look forward to bringing you many more in future years.

Mansfield Readers and Writers Committee 2023
Miriam Zolin, President
Margaret Attley OAM, Secretary
Leanne Allen, Treasurer
Alice Burton
Jennifer Chandler
Belinda Crawford
Lynn Elder
Dianne Williams

We acknowledge the Taungurung people as the original storytellers on the Country where this anthology was produced. We pay respect to the stories and the storytellers of First Peoples here and everywhere. Through our shared and separate stories, we heal, grow and connect.

Judge's Report
Laurie Steed

How do you write a great short story? Some days, I could not tell you, as there is so much a writer must do well for a story to hit its mark, including the creation of complex characters, a cohesive plot, and a genuinely engaging and even at times surprising narrative arc. On other days, specifics seem less important than the overall execution; in that space, a great story is far less tangible, the culmination of courage, depth, and necessary risk to write a story unlike anything that's previously been writing. Or perhaps I am being a little too fanciful here; perhaps uniqueness is too much pressure to put on any writer. With that in mind, let's go for different, original, and just a little ground-breaking in terms of its character, concept or conclusion.

The winning story of this year's local category was 'Love Thy Neighbour'. This story explores the tension in a suburban home when our protagonist is forced to listen to the dog next door being treated cruelly by its owner. There's real tension in that dilemma and the author deftly handles ethics surrounding when we step in, and why.

In the main category of this year's inaugural Mansfield Readers and Writers Competition there was one story that gripped me immediately and did not let up until a deeply satisfying ending to proceedings. That story, and this year's winning story, was 'Starry, Starry Cow,' and it is one of the best stories I've read in ages. While I'll leave you to read it for yourself, here, I'll just say that there's much you can do in a family story if you're willing to think outside of the box. In a story with this level of depth, there are many risks taken and surprise developments, and all pay off for what's one of the most rewarding, non-didactic female-empowerment stories I have ever had the pleasure to read.

Other shortlisted stories included 'Christmas Lights,' 'Roar,' and 'Thylacine'. 'Christmas Lights' merges the tropes of the festive season into something distinctly fresh and somehow still heart-warming. 'Roar' is a gut-punch of a story, tracking unimaginable loss through the surreal, the confronting, and the deeply heartbreaking. 'Thylacine', meanwhile, works in taut, beautifully stripped-back prose, tracking a man's attempts to rediscover the Tasmanian tiger, and a son who grows to see the significance of that quest. And, the aforementioned local prize-winner 'Love Thy Neigbour' also makes the shortlist for the main prize, such was its ability to take the reader into a familiar, believable moral conundrum.

If you submitted for the competition for this year and weren't shortlisted, my one suggestion would be to reduce your story scope while increasing risks taken on the page. Competitions are a cut-throat space. Those sitting on the fence are still working at their craft. Still, there's a much greater chance of success when you avoid the fence entirely, and instead are streaming across fields, arms held out, eyes wide, gazing skyward for the next burst of inspiration.

Laurie Steed, 2022

Starry Starry Cow
Deborah May

'Starry Starry Cow' is the winner of the inaugural Mansfield Readers and Writers short story competition.

Laura leans against the weatherboard wall of the house for support as she stands on one leg at a time, absent-mindedly flicking sand off her feet. She can still hear the squeals of teenagers jumping off the pier.

Jeff opens the door and looks at her with poorly concealed dismay. 'Hello! I didn't expect you back so soon.' He's freshly showered and dressed in the blue and white checked shirt she gave him for Christmas. Just that morning she'd taken it out of the gift bag where he'd left it for two weeks. The card was at the bottom, unopened. Stung by his ingratitude she'd been tempted to return the shirt, but instead she'd ironed the creases out of it and hung it up in his side–the tidy side–of the wardrobe.

'Too crowded down there for you, was it?'

Laura shrugs and steps past her husband into the cool hallway which still smells of festive pumpkin spice candles–a scent ridiculously at odds with the hot evening.

She doesn't tell Jeff that as she'd walked past clusters of people, clumsily stepping over the corners of beach towels and holes dug by kids with plastic shovels, she'd felt as if she radiated a toxic cloud of misery. The memory of spending evenings like this with Tom when he was a child had intensified Laura's sadness so much that her mouth wobbled and she couldn't work out how to control it.

Jeff bends down and picks up her thongs which she's left on the doormat. 'Here,' he says handing them to her, as if he's doing her a favour. He can't stand things out of place. 'I'm heading to the pub for a bit.' He runs his hands through his damp hair which is still fairly thick, thanks to a strict regimen of Rogaine and his laser hair cap.

It's easy to tell when Jeff's lying. Despite doing it so frequently, he's never really become any better at it. Laura, on the other hand, has become adept at pretending she hasn't noticed.

She drops her thongs in the hallway and watches from the lounge room window as Jeff climbs into his car and puts the top down before reversing through the narrow gap left by parked cars overlapping the driveway.

A steady stream of people pass the house on their way to the beach to catch the sunset. Laura has the all too familiar sensation of missing out on life while everyone else is living it.

'Right, then,' she says out loud into the semi-darkness, the surprise at this unexpected opportunity apparent in her voice. 'Let's get to work.'

Laura started talking aloud to herself when Tom was a baby as a way to help his language development and then she never stopped. She spent so much time alone after Tom went to school that when she did try to speak after not talking for hours her voice sounded guttural, like it was emerging from a deep tunnel. Sometimes the sound of her voice in the empty house shocks her, as if it's someone else speaking.

Her sweaty feet squeak on the floorboards. The golden light on the walls and the sound of the sprinklers whirring remind her of tiptoeing down the hall with Tom as a sleeping baby in her arms. Since Tom left for Sydney three days ago, the house seems full of ghosts of him at all the different stages he's passed through on his way to deserting her. After nineteen years of telling people who ask what she 'does' that she's a stay-at-home Mum, Laura has no idea how she's supposed to define herself going forward. She wonders if she's the only parent who somehow assumed that this day would never really come.

Jeff's iPad is in the front pocket of his leather work bag, as she knows it will be. He always returns it there, after carefully wiping down the screen with a microfibre cloth and closing its protective case.

She places his iPad on the desk in the study and connects it to her laptop with a USB cord. The window faces the street, so she'll see Jeff's car when he returns. Across the deep front lawn, faded in the middle where the sprinklers don't reach, the topiary roses bordering the garden cast long shadows.

Laura often feels as if their Federation style house is the fourth member of their family, that it listens to her when she talks aloud. Lately, it seems to expand and shrink as if by magic. It's too big and empty when she's here alone, now that all the belongings Tom leaves lying around are gone. Yet, when Jeff's home, it seems to contract, becoming suffocatingly small as the two of them try to work out how to live together without having Tom as a buffer.

Jeff's iPad is old and slow to get going. She picks up the only ornament on the desk–a porcelain cow, covered in the swirls of Van Gogh's Starry Night. Even though it's missing half a leg (broken in a move) and Jeff has asked more than once if he can throw it out, she's hung onto it.

'You bought it for me,' she reminded him the last time he mentioned it. 'It's sentimental.'

'I remember,' he'd said, pleased, placing it back on the desk. 'I just didn't know you did.'

She remembers Jeff withdrawing his hand from hers to pull out his wallet and pay for the cow at a museum shop. 'Your first souvenir of America,' he'd said, handing her the bag and kissing her head. It was in

Chicago at the end of 1999, during the Cow Parade exhibition, when decorated life-size fibreglass cows were scattered throughout the city.

So naive at twenty-two, she had thought those three months in Chicago were just the beginning of a romantic life of adventure. She had no idea that was the pinnacle.

Laura rubs her thumb over the rough white stump of the cow's broken left hind leg. The communal cicada drone amplifies her loneliness.

Tom rings as she's searching for her laptop charger. He's called a couple of times a day so far, which has gone a small way towards repairing the tear of his sudden departure.

'How are you going?' he asks. His concern both touches and irritates her.

'I'm fine, darl. How about you? Getting settled in?'

'Yeah,'

Laura can tell by his doubtful voice that his belongings are still piled up in the hallway of the furnished flat in Newtown, rented for him by Jeff without a murmur of complaint.

The question of why Tom moved interstate a month before his course at NIDA even begins hangs between them but she would never ask him to incriminate his father. Much better to hack into Jeff's iPad.

'What are you up to?' The homesickness in Tom's voice reminds her of the early days of primary school where he'd cling to her at drop-off. He'd had terrible separation anxiety. So had she. How hard it had been to force him back to the classroom instead of whisking him home.

'Nothing much, just went for a walk.' She wanders into the kitchen and opens the fridge. There's barely anything in there. Without her gangly son to feed, routines like grocery shopping seem pointless. There's some foil-wrapped Christmas leftovers lingering at the back of the fridge. Eventually Jeff will get hungry enough to investigate them and be confronted with whatever mysterious gunge is inside.

She pulls out a pear cider.

'Where's Dad?'

'At the pub. Do you want him to call you?'

'No. I was just wondering.'

'Are you sure you're okay?'

'Yeah Mum. I love you. Call me if you need anything.'

After she hangs up she exhales a loud sigh into the empty house as she twists the top off her cider.

Three days ago, in the driveway next to his Jeep laden with all his belongings, Tom had hugged her until she could surreptitiously wipe her black tears on his sleeve. He pretended not to notice, knowing she wanted to appear brave, enthusiastic. Yay! You're leaving home! Starting the next stage of your life! The ripping feeling in her heart was one she didn't know she was still capable of feeling.

Laura has no idea how Tom will manage to look after himself. He's like her, dreamy and disorganised. When Jeff tells Tom that he's just like his mother, they all know he doesn't mean it as a compliment. She'll visit Tom to help him settle in eventually, but she'll wait to be invited. She doesn't want Tom to know she doubts his capability.

Jeff used to find her messiness endearing. He must have–they were literally in the middle of her chaos, when he invited her to go to Chicago with him. They were in Laura's tiny damp flat, lying on her carpet stained with coffee and wine and littered with tram tickets and coins. She couldn't believe that this beautiful man wanted her to go away with him when they'd only been seeing each other for four weeks. Her last boyfriend was like Laura–a recent uni graduate living a temporary existence of stepping-stone jobs and casual living arrangements, as he tried to navigate the adult world.

Jeff's trip, to spend three months with his uncle in the Chicago branch of his family's corporate apparel and sportswear business, was planned long ago by his father. It was the final step before Jeff would take over the Melbourne branch of Coreletix.

How brave it was of him to invite her, especially in light of his recent divorce, Laura had thought. Later she realised that he hadn't been brave at all–he'd assessed her living situation and decided she had absolutely nothing to lose. Of course she'd say yes.

Laura's mother, widowed at thirty and living a life of negativity and bitterness ever since, was suspicious. 'You need to be careful of this man,' she'd warned. 'Something's not right.'

On her way back to the study from the kitchen, a banging on the front door gives Laura such a fright her arms shoot up and cider sloshes out of the bottle onto her feet and the floor. Her first thought is that it's Jeff. But Jeff wouldn't bang, he'd let himself in, hoping to slip through to the ensuite unnoticed.

Someone is trying the door handle.

'It's locked,' an unfamiliar male voice says.

'He's got to be home,' says another man. 'Where else would he be?'

The next round of banging sounds like someone is using the side of their fist. The framed family photos on the walls either side of the front door rattle. Her keys jangle in the metal tray on the hall stand.

'Come on, open the door.'

'Or I'm going to take a piss on the verandah.' A chorus of laughter. There must be at least four guys out there.

For years she's half-expected an angry spouse to turn up at their door, based on her suspicions about Jeff. But she never anticipated a mob.

Laura is only a few feet from the door. If the men step to the right and look in, they'll be able to see her from the lounge window. She has a sense of being outside her body, watching herself shuffle down the hall towards Tom's bathroom at the back of the house, where the only window is high up and made of frosted glass.

When she sits on the edge of the bath, she notices her knees wobbling. She stretches her leg and closes the door over with her foot.

How strange to find herself shut in here again.

The last time she hid in here, Tom's green size two dressing gown was hanging on that hook on the back of the door and the now empty bathroom had been littered with colourful bath toys. She'd kidnapped Jeff's Blackberry, and was reading text messages between him and Katie, a woman from sales. That was so hot, Jeff had texted the day before. You have so much passion, Katie had just responded. It was pure coincidence that Laura was checking Jeff's calendar to see what time the architect was arriving when the message from Katie came through.

'It was only a kiss,' Jeff insisted from the other side of the locked bathroom door. 'It didn't mean anything. She grabbed me.'

She'd emerged when the architect arrived, but not before dropping Jeff's Blackberry in the toilet and flushing. He'd fished it out but it hadn't worked again. He'd had the nerve to be angry about it, as if she was in the wrong.

She'd watched Jeff, as if seeing him for the first time as he discussed designs with the architect, seeming unconcerned by her silence. Tom sat on her lap, colouring with wind-up crayons and she clutched him to her as if he was a life buoy.

The white gravel path around the house crunches with the sound of the men's footsteps. They're passing by the bathroom now. Laura stays completely still.

'He must have gone to grab some beer or something,' someone says. 'His car's not here.'

The laundry door handle is rattled. 'Locked too.'

'Nice enough house,' says the guy with the deep voice. 'A lot smaller than I expected though.'

They never had renovated in the end. Some things just couldn't be fixed. They learned to live with small windows and cramped living spaces, one child instead of the three they'd originally planned. Of course they carried out some half-hearted repairs; repainted some rooms, attended some marriage counselling sessions.

Monique the marriage counsellor, an elegant older French woman, threw Jeff a lifeline when she suggested that, like so many men, he'd felt neglected once Tom was born. He grabbed that lifeline and hung on for dear life. Yes, he'd said to Laura, as Monique nodded in sympathy. If she'd been more attentive to him, more attentive to the state of the house even, he would never have been tempted. So really, he reassured Laura, who still so desperately wanted to believe in him, they were both at fault.

'The best way I can describe Katie is like this,' Jeff said during their third and final appointment, clasping his hands in front of him as if begging for understanding. 'She's like a porn magazine that I can just throw away.' He tossed an imaginary magazine toward the bin.

Laura saw her own feeling of revulsion reflected briefly on Monique's usually impassive face.

After that session, Jeff, always the driver in their relationship, declared it was time to move on. 'You're never going to get over it if you keep rehashing it,' he told her. 'We both just need to make more of an effort.'

She carried her heartbreak around as a heavy, guilty secret. She withdrew from her friends, who hoped to find a man as dependable as Jeff. She was unwilling to disillusion them but also unable to listen to them gush over him anymore.

Poor Tom, two years old at the time, became a lightning rod, drawing Laura and Jeff's attention away from each other onto him.

Laura waited to see what happened next, always imagining that one day clarity would arrive and she'd know what to do. She'd never been good at making decisions and the older she got, the more she doubted her ability to make good choices. She lived in a permanent state of watchfulness and suspicion, riddled with insecurities, because despite Jeff's promise to try harder, she felt increasingly invisible.

And here they all are, seventeen years later. They'd survived almost intact, until now.

The grey floor tiles in the bathroom are cracked and the paint on the roof is peeling. It smells damp, even this evening, with the slightly open window letting in the warm air. Tired of sitting on the edge of the bath, Laura climbs into the tub, brushing a couple of dead moths into the plug hole.

'Ah well. So we wait.' The men have finished their loop of the house and are back at the front door. There are the sounds of heavy things being put down on the verandah. Is it possible they brought weapons?

'Not too bad out here.' Laura hears the creaking of the wicker armchair as someone sits.

'I tell ya, he's gonna pay when he gets here, making us wait.'

She should warn Jeff. How will she tell Tom that she let his father be beaten to a pulp on the verandah? Well, he needed to be taught a lesson you know, she imagines saying. She pictures larger-than-life Jeff in the fetal position, covering his head. No, she doesn't want that to happen at all. People can die from just one punch. As much as she resents Jeff for all he's put her through, she does not want to see that.

She has to warn him.

But her phone is on the kitchen bench. If she goes to get it, one of the men will see her moving through the house in the darkness. Why risk her own safety when it's his behaviour that's brought them here? Why is she the one who always suffers the consequences of his actions?

Maybe they just want to have a chat to him. They sound harmless enough, although Laura's unable to listen to most of their conversation. She hears the cracking of beer can tabs as the men settle in to wait. 'Wish I'd brought some chips,' one of them says. 'I'm starving.'

She's certain now that something Tom saw in Jeff's office forced his hasty departure and that these guys may know what it is.

Jeff had hired Tom to create a new display for the showroom window. Tom hated going to Coreletix. 'Mum, there's nothing I can do to make those ugly uniforms look good,' he complained before he left.

A couple of hours later he stormed home and started packing, refusing to talk about it besides saying, 'Don't worry Mum, it's got nothing to do with you.'

When she'd asked Jeff what happened, he shrugged.'You know Tom–always unpredictable. I guess he just wants to get away from us.'

Curiosity getting the better of her, Laura went for a drive past the Coreletix office in Moorabbin. As she suspected, Tom's display in the large window facing the street had been abandoned, and the mannequins were half-naked. It looked like a unisex locker room scene.

It reminded her of how Jeff had discovered his first wife's affair with the finance officer all those years ago. He'd walked into a storage room full of mannequins and thought he was hallucinating when he saw the two of them writhing on the floor.

Googling, Why does my husband cheat? one day, Laura discovered an article entitled The Narcissist's Hidden Pain. It talked about how a narcissistic personality could be created by a traumatic event and how from that moment, the narcissist's behaviour was aimed solely toward obtaining validation from others. It was illuminating. Perhaps there was nothing she could have done differently after all–maybe their relationship had been doomed from the start by his first marriage.

She often wishes she'd never seen that text from Katie–perhaps then she could have been happy. Maybe she would be able to look at Jeff without that gnawing feeling of disappointment.

Looking back, Laura thought that she could have been anyone, that that there was nothing special about her, or their relationship at all. He'd probably proposed on the flight home from Chicago to get his life plan back on track after it being derailed by his first marriage. His ex-wife was just a faulty carriage, uncoupled and replaced as he steamed ahead.

At the end of November, Jeff and Laura had taken Tom to dinner to celebrate the end of his VCE exams. It all went smoothly until Tom went outside to take a call. Irritated, Jeff called the waitress over, a girl about Tom's age, to get yet another cocktail. As he ordered Jeff had actually reached out and put his large hand around the girl's bare forearm, tattooed with hibiscus flowers, as if she needed to be held there. Laura kicked him under the table but he ignored her. 'Why don't you tell me what I should have?' he asked the waitress as he looked at her with the same intense gaze that he used to rest on Laura.

How did he think it was okay to put his hand on a total stranger like that? Right in front of her? 'Keep your bloody hands to yourself!' she wanted to scream but she said nothing.

The waitress's smile didn't falter but she'd moved her arm and looked at Laura as if she was an irresponsible pet owner who'd let her untrained puppy off the leash.

A male waiter served them for the rest of the evening.

'I hate it when they change waiters mid-meal,' Jeff grumbled. He didn't leave a tip.

When they got home that night she'd looked at him sitting on the edge of the bath in his undies flossing his teeth. She felt insulted that he didn't mind her seeing him sitting like that, hunched over, his hairy grey chest melting into his burgeoning beer gut, making her think of the characters from the Barbapapa books she'd read as a child. There are times when she remembers not being able to keep her hands off him and it makes her want to cry.

That night in bed, Laura had actually felt sorry for him. She'd spooned up behind him, thinking that for someone who was so dependent on female admiration, growing old was going to be rough.

Since then, Laura wonders about the high female staff turnover at Coreletix; if at times Jeff wrongly assumes his own attraction to someone is reciprocated. Sometimes he looks like a young boy excited about going to school when he leaves for work in the morning, and there are also days he comes home dejected like a dumped teenager.

Laura avoids going to Jeff's office as much as possible, but when she does–usually because she's locked herself out of the house–she feels like people are whispering about her, watching with a mixture of pity and disdain as she ascends the metal staircase up to Jeff's office. She leaves with the sense that they know more about her husband than she does.

Of course it could all be her imagination. It's the not knowing what's real and what's paranoia that kills her.

She thinks of Jeff's iPad tethered to her laptop.

The night Tom left, devastated that Jeff had robbed her of her last month with her son, she decided it was time. She needs hardcore proof, something Jeff can't lie his way out of. When Jeff pulled out his iPad that night, as usual, complaining about being behind on work emails, she stood behind him under the pretence of closing the curtains and watched him type in his passcode.

Last night, noticing Jeff peeking furtively at her every now and then as he tapped away, she'd purchased software that promised, for $149.95, to recover any deleted texts, photos and WhatsApp messages.

It's dark now and cars are leaving the street; there's a near constant sound of closing car doors and engines starting.

I am a fool, Laura thinks. Why does she feel ashamed in a way that Jeff himself doesn't? It's as if because she's married to him, that she's complicit in his behaviour. Here she is hiding in a bath when the answer to what she wants to know is literally on her doorstep. It's so typical. Her desire to know the truth has always been outweighed by her terror of the facts. Unlocking her arms and legs she stiffly climbs out of the bath.

Laura marches down the dark hall and pulls the front door open. Four men look up surprised. One of them who'd been sitting with his back against the door nearly falls inside the hallway against her legs.

He scrambles to his feet, a stocky man in a yellow polo shirt, kicking over a Guinness can. Frothy beer dribbles across the verandah.

'Norm?' he asks sheepishly.

'Norm?' Laura repeats and they all look at each other in confusion.

A phone pings and the skinny red-haired man in the deck chair stands up to pull his phone from his pocket. 'Oh shit!' he exclaims. 'We're at the wrong bloody house. He's at 93, not 39. He just texted me to ask where we were.'

They gather up their beer and apologise profusely as they back away across the lawn. They step over the low fence and onto the footpath. It's only when they reach the street and disappear into the darkness that they burst into raucous laughter. She hears one of them ask, 'So, was she in there the whole time?'

The idea that the mob she's been hiding from has materialised into that group of buffoons is disconcerting. Yet again her imagination has got the better of her. Laura stands on the verandah and looks up at the deep blue sky which is full of stars.

She's sickened by herself, to think she's disappointed that they weren't there to confront Jeff. 'This is the kind of person Jeff has turned you into.' The house maintains a disapproving silence.

Laura's feet are sticky. On the way to the door she's walked through the patch of cider she spilled earlier.

As she looks down at her feet she thinks of how, in the early days, Jeff would fetch her a pair of his ski socks if he noticed her feet were cold. He'd tenderly put them on her feet. He loved her feet, he'd said.

This is always what happens. Whenever she thinks she's reached the end of their relationship, she goes right back to longing for the beginning.

She closes the front door and walks down the dark hall to the study.

We have recovered 13,234 messages, 270 photos, 1345 WhatsApp messages' the text on her screen says. Would you like to download?

Laura clicks 'Yes' and sits mesmerised for what seems like an eternity in the dark, watching the blue bar move slowly across the screen. A cool breeze seeps in from the sash windows. Little black insects settle on her computer.

She traces her finger over Tom's name, scratched into the bottom left corner of the wooden desk. As soon as he learned to write he'd put his name everywhere he could reach. It had driven Jeff nuts. Laura smiles.

It makes her feel as if Tom is here with her. She wishes so much that she could walk down to his room and look at a little toddler version of him sleeping.

Laura picks up the porcelain cow as her laptop completes its task of extracting Jeff's secrets. For so long she's kept this cow on her desk as a reminder that Jeff loved her once. She hoped it would prompt her towards forgiving him. But really, it's just a stupid, broken, ugly cow.

Her whole body aches with a pain starting in her chest as she starts to scroll.

When Jeff comes home at 2 am Laura's waiting for him.

'What's this?' he asks, glancing at her puffy eyes and turning away to drop his keys into the dish on the hall stand. 'I thought you'd be in bed.'

'Some men came to the house,' she said.

'Who?'

'I thought they were here to see you. I thought it was about someone you'd got mixed up with.'

'What did they look like?' His hands plunge into his hair. 'What did they tell you?'

'It doesn't matter. Come here.'

'I've got to have a quick shower. It was stinking hot in the pub.'

He tries to slip past her, but she grabs him and buries her face into his chest. 'Just wait a minute,' she says with uncharacteristic authority.

She remembers how safe she used to feel listening to his slow and steady heartbeat. Right now, it's beating quickly, like an animal under threat. His body is tense at first, resisting, but then it collapses. She feels his shoulders slump. His arms reach around her and hold her to him, against the shirt she gave him that smells so strongly of another woman's perfume.

It would be so easy to just stay there, pretending none of this is happening.

Until he says, 'Whatever you're thinking, I can promise you, it's not true.'

She steps back and looks at his flushed face. He looks old, the lines on his forehead deep as he frowns down at her, his brown eyes slightly bloodshot. She wonders if in the future he'll think that the last couple of hours was worth this.

She could tell him about the incriminating messages and photos she recovered between him and various women, including Katie, now an older but still attractive woman. But why give him the chance to make excuses and find a way to blame her? She is done with punishing herself.

'Tom's grown up,' she says, thinking of the cruellest thing she can say. 'I don't have to pretend to love you anymore.'

She squeezes his arm before stepping past him, closing the front door behind her. She walks across the damp lawn to her car parked on the street. Her bags are already inside it.

Laura sees him in the study, drawn there because she's left the light on. He picks up his iPad, the USB cord dangling. Now he's probably noticing her name that she carved into the desk next to Tom's.

In a moment he'll see the little blue cow at the bottom of the wastepaper pin, its remaining three legs snapped off, but she doesn't stay to watch.

Judge's Comments

'Starry Starry Cow' may have a quirky title but the story is anything but. The tale of a wife and mother making necessary life-changing decisions, it's also a fantastic meditation on fear and existential anxiety, and much more besides. Indeed, to literally describe this story is a bit like telling somebody that Anthony Doerr and Alice Munro write great stories, when really, the greater context of what's achieved, and how, is much more spectacular. While comparisons to Doerr or Munro are high-praise, it would be tough to argue that the scope of the narrative is not in line with the former writer's work, or that the emotional depth of this story does not mirror the latter.

This story is written with supreme faith in both the strength of its unfolding narrative, and also in the reader. Indeed, stories like this remind me why I love to judge competitions in the first place. If you are looking to work out why a certain story wins a competition, then this is a great place to start. One enters its fictional world innocuously, dipping one's toes into the story before realising soon enough it's not a pool, it's an ocean. Character-based storytelling does not get any better than this.

Love Thy Neighbour
Sinead Reilly

'Love Thy Neighbour' is the local writer winner of the inaugural Mansfield Readers and Writers short story competition.

1

I'm not sure what time it is. Late. I can tell because I can't hear any cars passing by. I usually can. Shadows of the tree outside my window are spilling across my ceiling. I can hear nothing save for the wind.

I concentrate on trying to lie perfectly still in the dark. I can't remember it ever being this dark.

I am starting to feel as though I am floating in a tank when I register the first yelp. An animal. I think it's a cat, but upon hearing it again, it's clearly a dog. Must be my neighbour's dog–the young guy a bit further up. Don't know his name. The place that separates our houses has been vacant for a time. A nice young couple lived there long enough to realise they probably needed better. That was about a year ago, and the 'For Sale' sign is still up. Sunburnt now, peeling round the edges, and the photos are all faded too.

I try to listen more closely. The shadows continue to gambol about on the ceiling. If I don't blink, they get bigger and bigger.

After a few minutes I hear another whine. It's not really a whine, but I don't know how else to describe it. I haven't heard anything like it. I don't want to believe that it's a dog making that sound. A flurry of barks every so often means I can't fool myself much longer. The neighbours on the other side don't have any pets. Just the one guy there alone for as long as I've been here and probably twenty years more. I shouldn't be able to hear the dog from here.

Only minutes have passed before I hear it again. And again. The furiously dancing patterns, faster and faster, falling into and over each other–extricating contorting unfolding–transfix my sight in the still dark. Again. I shut my eyes.

I try to think of the last time I saw the dog. Can't think of her name, or how she looked. I know she's a retriever, white gold one. I like those ones. The yellow ones are alright. I can't think of whether I ever asked her name or how old she is or when the neighbour brought her home or anything much at all, not even what he looks like. Around my height maybe. Closing my eyes hasn't done much good at all. It's still going.

2

When I wake, the birds outside my window are calling to each other. They sound listless this morning. Feeble. They're probably not because birds can't really be listless or feeble unless they're sick or dying but maybe they can be. An ex-girlfriend of mine kept a parrot that always looked sort of miserable. Pulled out a bunch of its feathers once. She said it was stressed. I ended up letting it out the window and it probably didn't last much longer after that.

The sky is strewn with watery ink and some thin clouds, and acid from my stomach coats the back of my throat.

Fast-forward three blank months and I can remember little else but the sound of the dog getting kicked–which now seems optimistic–half to death every Friday night. I don't know why it only happens on Fridays. I don't think there is a reason. The guy could just clock off work and go have some beers like everyone else, but that doesn't seem to be on his agenda.

Strewn between the melting months have been increasingly desperate attempts to get a hold of someone at the police station that won't promise a call back and then not call back.

I get through.

I don't want to fixate on what the woman sounded like, or even what she said when I asked why they haven't been answering the phone. I don't even think I asked. Not important. I was just happy that someone finally picked up. The voice–Carolina, I wrote it down–informed me that two officers will visit my neighbour's house on Thursday.

Today is Sunday.

I told her that the dog gets beat up on Fridays–a visit on Thursday might be too late. What if he's not home, what if he's at work or the supermarket or takes his car to the mechanic, he has a job, he works, it's a nine to five job and that's all I know, I haven't spoken to the guy much but he does work and he goes out after work too, he really isn't home that much but I also don't know because I don't keep tabs on what the guy does at every waking moment but maybe I should if they can't arrange to visit after five or earlier in the week.

Carolina asks me to please calm down. She's chewing gum. I want to hang up but there's a good chance that the dog would be in the ground by the time I manage to get through again.

I say thank you, make sure the officers do visit, thank you and goodbye.

Pieces of broken glass swim innocently in water on my kitchen floor. It's spattered all over the bit of paper I'd written my neighbour's address on. I watch as the letters bleed into each other slowly. It's sodden. I don't remember smashing the glass.

Trying not to think about the retriever, I pick up the slivers of glass and clean the water up. Snowy white fur matted with dark blood. My hands are shaking a little. Big soft ears.

3

Today is Thursday, and I've taken the day off work. Predictably, my neighbour is gone already. I need a day off anyway. I pace around my house and yard, caged, waiting for the officers to turn up.

I wait all day.

At around three, a flock of schoolgirls glide down the street. Snatches of their laughter float in through my windows.

They don't show up.

4

I wake in the early hours of Friday morning to the shrieks of the dog. My neighbour has tweaked his schedule slightly. Rest and recuperation. I lie in bed awhile with some music turned up full volume, trying not to picture violent things happening to him.

Getting into my car, I drive through the night until the hard dark sky is tempered a little by the dawn. Settling on radio voices talking about nothing much in particular, I turn the volume up to maximum and put all the windows down. The cool wind whips through the car and stays with me and I can't hear the voices talking at me at all.

Eventually I pull over by someone's field. The house is all dark and far away.

Ducking through the barbed wire fence, I lie down in the long grass. The ground has been softened by rain and I know I'm not meant to be here and the owners could come out at any minute but I'm just having a lie-down and I don't mind saying that I just like the look of their field but I have to get back in time for work and now the sunrise is coming up all ooh-la-la pink and topaz and it's beautiful but the retriever's ears and snowy bloody fur do not leave.

5

Friday night proves something of a respite. Wonder what's up with him.

The following morning, I wait for him to go to work. He's listening to some pop rubbish as he drives away. The wailing voices probably help drown out his conscience if he ever had one.

Tucking some old blankets under my arm, I turn down the narrow pathway leading to his backyard from the street. I didn't know how many I'd need so I brought them all. The front gate is abnormally small, so I push it open with my foot. I let myself into the backyard via the cracked path beside the house.

It takes me a few minutes to find her. She's in the shed and can't walk on her own. I think a fair few of her bones must be broken. Gingerly, I wrap her up in the blankets and she whines with pain when I pick her up off the stained concrete. She's feather light, much too light, and I'm sorry, I'm sorry, I'm sorry. Liquid brown eyes look up at me as I carry her down the street with soft steps and I swear I've never seen anything look at me so bleakly. The pavement feels warm under my feet, radiating through my shoes and into my legs. I feel dizzy.

The vet pointedly asks a lot of questions. I don't blame him. She now sports some fresh blue bandages.

Later, at home, I carefully wash her snowy fur more carefully than I'd wash a newborn. I'm lathered up to my chest in red soapy foam. I towel her dry, smiling beatifically all the while. I even hum a little bit. I can't help it.

After a couple of days go by, my neighbour knocks on the door. One-two-three.

I briefly consider ignoring it, but I know I should answer it. I don't want him to get any ideas. If I don't answer it, he might go round the back.

His hair is matted to his forehead, and his eyes are all filmy organza. I instantly want to close the door in his face. He's got one of those smiles where you can see all the teeth, a bit like that first witch in *The Witches*– the movie they made out of the Roald Dahl novel. That scene scared the fuck out of me, mostly because of all her teeth and her throaty needle-filled voice. *What a magnificent treehouse*, she drawls. I'm never going to watch that movie again in case the scene is ruined for me. I don't think this guy is going to compliment my non-existent treehouse but my point is that he doesn't look right.

He tells me where he lives, as if I didn't know, and asks whether I've seen the dog. I think a moment before shaking my head. I tell him I'll keep an eye out.

Yes, he says. Please do. He hasn't blinked this whole time.

I close the door and turn around.

The dog has a well-what-the-hell-happens-now look on her face. I don't know but I don't feel worried.

Judge's Comments

'Love Thy Neighbour' is a story that knows the power of proximity. When that proximity is next-door, then the stakes are immediately high. This story does not once shy away from its central conflict, and therein lies its real strength. For a fine first-person short story is, if nothing else, a study in being emotionally stuck, for whatever reason. In this story our protagonist eventually finds a way out, and it's with that courage to act that, as readers, we are able to really get behind this story. It's a simple but raw piece of storytelling and one that deeply benefits from its believable, timely subject matter of pets, and the responsibility inherent, but so often lacking in the people who own them.

Held by the Sea
Molly Dunn

The story submitted by this young, local writer impressed the committee of Mansfield Readers and Writers. We decided to acknowledge the entry and its author with an encouragement award. Congratulations Molly, and we look forward to reading many more of your stories.

'Stay. Please stay.'

His young voice gently parts the silence, heard by none but I. I press my body harder into the sandbank, trying, once again, to hear the heartbeat. His words aren't for me, for I am invisible to him, much to my regret. Rather, he speaks to the tide. To the sand, to the sun, already dipping its head behind a veil of black. Soon, his mother will come looking, as I am sure she has been, for her boy, fearful of his wanderings. She can't know that he isn't alone; that I am here with him. I'm invisible to her, too.

'Don't leave,' it comes a second time, and his hand reaches down, over the sandbank, stretching for the sea.

Stumbling footsteps followed by a sharp sigh. His mother makes her way along the shore, sand spraying as she hurries for her strange son.

'How many –' another sigh, this one of resignation. Every night she scolds him, and each night finds her back here.

'Just–just come on, quickly. I've got the dinner on and your father is– you know how he is. Dust yourself off, there you go, now.'

I watch as her hand wraps around his thin arm, pulling him from the edge of the shelf and towards home. He allows himself to be dragged along, but his eyes never leave the horizon. He places his free hand over his heart, then touches it to his lips in prayer. I wait until they're out of sight, then push up from my crouch, brushing sand from my clothes. I picture his face again, the memories, old and new, of his fingers against his lips, his eyes wide in rapture, and I shiver. So strange, I think to my-self. Such a strange boy.

I paused before the door, hand hovering above the handle. Every night, this internal battle. If I leave now, I could go anywhere I want, haunted by guilt and loneliness; but if I enter, will I find the strength to leave again? My struggle is ended as the door opens from the inside. My sis-ter stands there, wiping flour off her face.

'Jesus, Keavy. Mum's in a huff, she sent the boys out to look for you. What's so important that you couldn't be back sometime before dark?'

She doesn't bother to wait for my answer, pulling me into the house. With her free hand she nudges the door closed, the other keeping the bowl wedged against her hip.

'What're we having, then?' I ask, reaching for the bowl. She spins away, her laughter too sharp, too loud after the softness of the night.

'Oh no you don't,' she teases, leading me into the kitchen. 'Give Mum a hand with the onions, you know she can't –' her instructions are cut off by a gasp as our mother rushes towards us.

'Oh, Keavy, look at the state of you, get yourself cleaned up before your father comes home, goodness…' she trails off, bustling me in the direction of my room. I smile, but it's forced, unnatural, and I turn my head before they notice.

'Yes, Mum.'

I twist the faucet, letting the bath fill as I slip from my clothes. Spring, now, but still early enough for the air to have a chill that cannot be warded off by even the thickest of layers. Lowering myself into the bath, I sigh, frustrated. One day, I promise myself. I'll find a place near the sea, where I know no one; where I can be a ghost, forever invisible, forever happy. Far away, a door opens, and men's voices fill the house, demanding and loud. One day. One day.

I watch as the moon climbs higher and higher, before gravity wraps its arms around it and pulls it back towards earth. Thoughts rear and muddle, too many to focus on a single one, so that they become background noise, impossible to quiet. I waited until my brothers and father had eaten before I left my room, unwilling to see the disappointment on their faces. Why, they would ask. I did not know why. Indoors held little allure for me, but the muddied wallaby tracks and quiet, hidden pockets of salt water, abandoned by the sea, held a wonder for me greater than I could comprehend. And the boy, of course. In the month since he had moved here, I'd followed him as a shadow would, unnoticed. His mind, however young, gave voice to my wonder. *The earth's heartbeat*, he'd whispered to my brothers, when they'd gone to offer housewarming gifts to our new neighbours—*can you feel it?* They'd barely contained their ridicule, rushing home to tell us of the strange boy, embellishing their story until the rest of us shook with laughter. I'd seen him, the next day, standing on the sandbar with his arms outstretched to the sea. Picking my way amongst the dead wood and debris that littered the beach, I'd made my way over to him, curious. He'd turned before I'd worked the courage to approach, his young face wiser than any I'd seen before. His hair was as long as a girls', and tangled, held back by a strip of fabric. And his eyes—at first, they frightened me, and I would've run had I not been so enraptured. Grey-faded grey, pale as driftwood, as smoke. I shuddered at the wrongness of them. But I had to ask about the heartbeat he spoke of.

'Is it true?' I'd asked, lowering my eyes to avoid his driftwood gaze. 'Can you really feel its heart?'

He opened his mouth to reply, then closed it. Cleared his throat.

'Not in the way you imagine,' he'd replied, his young voice clear. 'But I know it's there. It's…a song. A pulse. I feel it when the tide comes in, and when the sun breaks the clouds after rain. I lose it, sometimes. The earth goes quiet. Those are the times I am completely alone.'

My earlier apprehension dissipated, and I moved closer, relieved to have found someone who understood.

'Show me,' I'd whispered, but he was already turning away.

'I can't.' He'd said, and my stomach had filled with ice. 'I can't teach you to feel something that should be as obvious as breathing. If you can't feel it, you won't.'

The ice spread to my veins, to my mind, and I stood there, numb, unable to move as I watched him walk away.

Fate seemed intent on amplifying my shame, for I saw the boy many times throughout the next week. In town, or working alongside my brothers as they moved the herds from one paddock of dead grass to the next. No matter where I saw him, he acted as though I was already forgotten. I got into the habit of hiding my face around him, which only angered me further. Here was a child of nine, maybe ten years, and I was allowing myself to be embarrassed by a single shameful encounter. I tricked myself into believing that my shame was, in fact, hatred–and for a time, I was completely convinced that this strange boy was no more than a pretentious child.

Sleep was evading me once again. I had overheard my parents arguing, their cruel, blunt words driving me from the house. Before I realised where I was going, I found myself down by the shore. Kneeling in the shallows, I let the salt of my tears mingle with the sea, until they were one and the same. The waves played with tendrils of my hair, spreading them in a halo about me. I held myself perfectly still, unwilling to interrupt. Then I heard his voice.

'Stay,' I whipped my head around, the small movement creasing the water around me. He was facing towards my direction, hand outstretched towards the horizon. He wasn't looking at me, and I decided, impossibly, that he hadn't seen me yet. Careful not to move too quickly, I crawled from the shallows and pressed myself against the sandbank.

Sleep found me in the early hours of the morning, my dreams of faded grey eyes, framed by the sand and twisting moonah trees. I woke before the rest of the house, and, slipping outside, grabbed the shovel from its place beside the door. The embrace of the frost brought shivers down my neck, and I swung the shovel idly on my way to the orchard. Shaking the branches to remove the lower-hanging fruit–and using the shovel to pry it from the higher limbs–I made quick work of my chores, but chose to hang around the orchard a little longer. I dropped to my knees and lay back against the base of a dying pear tree, watching as the boy made his own rounds of his parents' orchard, some way up the hill. He was slower, and so had a habit of getting up earlier. At some point, I'd begun doing the same.

'Um, Keavy?'

I jumped, startled. A giggle greeted me, before a round, sunbrowned face pushed its way into my line of sight. I suppressed a sigh, and grinned at my friend.

'Hey, Bridget.'

She hunkered down beside me, stretching her legs across mine.

'God, it's freezing. What are you doing just sitting here, you'll catch your-oh.'

Her line of sight followed mine, and I watched as she noticed the boy knocking fruit from the trees.

'Him again? Really Keavy? He's, like, five years younger than you. It's creepy.'

I closed my eyes, trailing my fingers along the white frost–lace that blanketed the grass. Tiny crystals lodged beneath my fingernails, and I flicked them out, letting them melt into my palms.

'Keavy? Did you hear me?'

'Yes, Bridget.' I kept my eyes closed, focusing all my attention on the cold kisses along my skin. 'I've told you already. I don't like him like that, or at all, really. I just…find him interesting.'

A snort of disbelief came from my friend, before she made her way to her feet.

'Well, I hope that's the case. Are you coming over later? Ma's made teacake.'

I nodded absently, wiping my palms on my thighs. Bridget's family had been our closest friends in the years since we'd moved here, and I couldn't remember a time without her. She considers herself my saviour, the only thing keeping me from being a social outcast. I think she just enjoys having me all to herself. Either way, our friendship is mostly superficial. I think, if it came down to it, we'd both choose our own company over each other's.

The boy looks up, straight at me, and raises his hand briefly. It's nothing. But my heart swells.

'Bridget, honey, you look fabulous, where's–ah, Keavy. Come now, let's get out of their hair, it's almost teatime, hon.'

I give Bridget a hug and follow my mother out the door, shoving my feet into sandals before the damp ground seeps between my toes. A phalarope flies low above the trees, and I trace its path to a flock making their way along the river. The sight of the bird, so free and unrestrained, brings a smile to my lips. Beautiful, so beautiful.

'Mm,' my mother lets out a sound of appreciation beside me. 'White bird in a grey cardigan, my darling. My mum used to call them birds of mourning.'

I watch as the phalarope touches the surface of the river, breaking it. Settled in, it seems so natural that it was there–how could it be anywhere else?–even though I had just watched it graze the clouds. It belongs, I thought to myself.

How must it feel to belong so completely?

I find myself looking forward to the half–light before the dark, when the sun and moon look each other in the eye. It is a time when I'm easily able to slip away, to wait for the boy below the sandbar.

The morning greets me with raised voices. I lie there, trying to block them out, until they become screaming. Followed by a crash. I lurch for the door, running out into the kitchen. There, I see my parents facing one another, tears streaming down their faces. A plate lies, shattered, on the floor, and I stare at it to avoid looking at them. At the irreparable crack in my family. At some point, my sister and brother must have entered the kitchen, but all I know is that everyone was frozen, not daring to breathe too loudly lest it destroy us. Make a fool of our memories. Of our life. Our parents turned away, eventually–my mother falling into my sister's arms, my father leading my brothers out into the yard. The sound of wheels on gravel replaces the silence, and I shudder.

'Keavy,' my mother whispers, finally noticing me standing in the doorway of the kitchen, still staring at the broken plate. I refuse to look, to move.

'Keavy, baby, come here. It's okay. We'll move to the city, I'll find a job. We'll be happy.'

Her voice breaks, and I feel as though I'm breaking with it. The city? I would be too far from the sea–it would forget me–oh god. Oh god. Panic rises up within me, and I can't breathe, can't think around it. So I run.

I stumble over and over as I race towards the sea. Tears fill my eyes, and I swallow them down, choke on them. So many thoughts, so many faded sensations. I hit the water at a sprint, the momentum carrying me forward until I'm face–down in the waves. I finally let my tears fall, feeling the salt water fill my eyes, my nose, my lungs, until a burning starts in my chest. A thought, fleeting, that I should raise my head, that I need to draw breath, before I'm lost once again in the muted quiet of the ocean, in the comfort of its embrace. It holds me, gently, asking nothing in return, and for the first time in my memory I feel completely at peace. I don't have to leave the sea. I don't have to leave. As I lie there, cradled by the waves, a new kind of darkness tattoos the edges of my vision, staining it black. Even in the muddled state of my mind, I'm able to recognise it as dying. I'm dying. This thought is accompanied by something like surprise, before it's stifled by the comfort of the ocean. Death. It doesn't seem so scary up close. My heart stutters, and a breath escapes me, bubbles rising up, up, until they burst around my head like a thousand tiny fireworks. My pulse stutters again, slowing now. And as my heartbeat fades into the sea, a new, stronger reverberation echoes it. Overtakes it. It thrums through my body, resonating to the deepest recesses of my mind, my soul. Life, singing its last goodbye. The sea's heartbeat. My heartbeat.

Thylacine

Cassie Hamer

Mum's chopping onions, again. She holds a piece to her nose. Closes her eyes. I'm at the door, still smelling of travel

'Mum.'

Eyelids dart open. 'Sorry, love. I didn't hear you.' She lays the knife flat, wipes her hands on the tea towel as if she's been caught doing something unclean. 'Dinner'll be soon.'

'Where's Dad?'

'In the shed. He's going out.'

I stop, tap the door frame. 'You okay?'

Two years ago, I wouldn't have thought to ask because everything about a home seems normal, until you leave it.

'Just the onions.' She smiles.

It's always just the onions.

'It's so nice to have you home.' She kisses my cheek and I smell the salty brine of her tears.

He's in there, rattling round like a five-cent coin in a moneybox.

'Dad, it's me.' I press my hand into the smooth cool of the tin door. 'Dad?'

Squeal of metal on metal as he wrenches it open. Eyeballs me with blank irises, pupils like bullet holes. Zero recognition.

'It's me. Sam.'

Three seconds, then his eyebrows separate. Head jerks back. 'Sammy, so it is.' He taps my shoulder, takes in my hair. 'You look like a bloody hippy.' He sighs, gets back to his cage.

'Mum says you're going out.'

Oil and dirt, the straw smell of long-cut grass. Windows, plastered with newspaper clippings that are fading with age, like a fast-dying sun. I can recite those headlines like a poem.

New Footage Fuels Long Futile Hunt for Tasmanian Tiger

Ellendale Tiger Sighting Revealed as a Hoax

Scientists Pin Hopes on Cloning Tassie Tiger

'*I don't think it was a Tiger, I know it was...*'

'So, are you?'

'None of her bloody business.'

He goes back to yanking bits of metal around the shed.

'How about you go later? Have dinner first?'

When he slams down the gate on the wire cage it cracks and rolls like thunder and I hate myself for flinching at what I knew was coming.

'Dad, c'mon. I'm only here for the weekend. Take the night off.' I jam my hands into my jeans pockets and press them to my hip bones as Dad goes for the carving knife, the one he sharpens every time he goes. He checks the blade, this way and that, then looks back to me with eyes like metal filings.

'Don't pretend with me.'

Twelve years ago. Me and Dad in the ute, jouncing home along the dirt track back from the lake. Prawns on our fingers. Gutted fish in the esky. The promise of trout for dinner. I'm nine and Dad is still the age of legend.

In falling light and out of nowhere, he slams on the brakes. Cuts the ignition.

'What is it? A roo?' I put my knuckles under my bum to get a better view.

A finger to his lips. We watch. Wait. A creature crosses the trail ahead. A moment that's faster than a heartbeat. Something like a wolf, or a wild dog. Are there stripes? The dusk won't tell.

But Dad knows. His lips curl back over his teeth.

'Well I'll be.' He whistles under his breath.

'What, Dad? Whad'ya see?'

'Jesus bloody christ.' He looks at me. 'You saw it, didn't you? That was it. That was bloody it.' His eyes have a wildness, a joy that scares me. He squeezes the steering wheel like he's choking it. 'You saw it, didn't you Sammy? The stripes?'

He looks at me and his desperation has a peaty smell.

'I saw it, too, Dad. I saw it.'

For the rest of the drive, he talks like a typewriter. At home, he shows me photos. His scrapbook. He's even got a video of the last one, Benjamin, walking restlessly up and down the wire fence. Died of neglect, says Dad. Left out in the cold one night by a slack-arse zookeeper.

He borrows one of my exercise books to write a detailed record. Where we were. The time. The stripes. The distinctive stiff tail. And when he asks me if I want to sign it, I say *Yes, Dad* and I love how he squeezes my shoulder when I've finished.

That night, when I dream, I replay the whole thing in my head and this time, it's not a fox or a dog or a wolf that walks across the trail, it's definitely Benjamin. And it's like my memory is water that shape-shifts to fulfill whatever space needs filling.

In the days after, Dad rings the local paper and tells his mates what he's seen. That he knows it's out there. He knows. And they'll laugh and say *Good on ya Kev.* And Dad'll look at me and wink, because I saw it too. It's our thing, and none of his boofhead mates can take that away from him, from us.

But we never see another one again. Not together.

'Tell your mother we're going fishing and we'll be back late.'

'But we gave the rods away. When I went to uni?'

He looks at me like I'm a curious museum piece, one he's never seen before, then he smiles out of the side of his mouth. 'At uni, are ya?'

'Nearly three years.'

I want to tell him what it's like–how I'm now so used to living in a big city where the air is smoggy but glides in and out of my lungs like a swing and how the big blue ocean at the city's doorstep doesn't frighten me like the dry, spare paddocks at home and the chaotic bush that imprisons them. Open spaces aren't all created equal, I have learned.

Eight years ago. I'm 13 and my voice twangs like a beginner playing violin. Life is like swimming in a warm pool with the odd cold current - just a patch to get through. But it's getting harder and the cool patches are blooming like blood through a bandage. My mates are starting to notice things, notice Dad and it's the barbs that make me shiver.

On a school excursion to the big Hobart Museum, we get to visit the basement. Jars and jars of pickled specimens. Ghostly foetuses, caught in limbo. Paws pressed to the glass. Jaws, wide and hungry.

In one of the jars is a baby Thylacine, white as bone and no bigger than a mouse. Eyes that never opened. Paws that never touched the ground. A brain that never knew fear. Never understood what it was like to be hunted by the territorial farmer.

Next to the foetus is another jar that contains a Thylacine heart, the size of a Tombola marble. It's small but perfect. The label says it's very similar to a human's–four chambers in all - left and right atrium, left and right ventricle. I press my forehead to the glass and cup my hands to eliminate my reflection, stare at the heart until my eyes start to sweat. I blink, blink again and the tiny organ starts to pulse, like a star twinkling in the dark.

You're not fully gone, not yet.

The next time Dad asks me to go trapping, I say yes straight away.

The bellies of the clouds rest on the hills. The bush is cemetery-quiet. Dad chooses the spots for the trap. He stops, nose to the wind.

'I can smell them.' He looks around. 'They're here.'

'Dad, they're not. You know that.'

'Course they bloody are. They're everywhere. Place is crawling with them.'

'Dad—' I start and stop. 'Dad, there aren't any. There's none. They're gone.'

'You don't know that,' he growls.

'But I do. I do know that. And so do you.'

He looks at me with hatred. And I'm waiting in silence and the moment crackles, like that gap when you count the seconds between lightning and thunder. But then he shifts, blinks, goes to the cages like I never said a thing. Like I wasn't trying to crush him.

'C'mon, you just gonna bloody stand there.'

After, we drive home in silence. Dad's eyes are fixed ahead. Hands pressed to the wheel. He's in there, somewhere, floating in pickling liquid.

In the morning, Mum's fussing about with rags and their bedroom smells of urine. Dad snores away on the couch.

'He forgot where the toilet was,' whispers Mum. 'Didn't even know me.'

We carry the mattress into the sun and I want to tell her she doesn't need the onions today. She doesn't need to pretend.

'He seems fine now,' I say. 'Don't worry.'

'You'll have to go and check the traps.' Mum wipes her hands. 'He was worrying about them last night.'

'I'll go after lunch. I'm meeting Stu at the pub.'

'That's good, love,' she says with hope. Yesterday, I told her I was thinking about staying in Sydney after graduation, trying to get an internship at one of the big accounting firms there. An hour later, she was chopping onions.

Mum goes on. 'You two were peas in a pod, back in the day. You must miss him.'

'Yeah,' I say. 'Be really good to see him.'

'How's uni?' Stu's hand clasps protectively around the pot like he's worried I'm going to take a cheeky swig, which is something I might have done a few years ago.

'Yeah, good. Pretty easy. Six months and I'm done.' To describe my city life to him feels like trying to describe a sunset. There just aren't the words and what's the point anyway? 'How's the farm?'

'Could do with some rain but we'll be right.'

We reach for our beers. Stu's bashed-up akubra takes up most of the table. In the background the barman polishes glasses. Waits for more customers. At midday on a Saturday, the pub is as empty as the sky, with only the aromas of beer and cigarettes to trouble it.

I lower my voice. 'Remember how hard we used to try to get into this joint? The fake ID? What were we thinking? It's a shit hole.'

'I've still got mine.' Stu produces his wallet.

'Christ, that photo makes you look like Freddie Mercury.' Both of us crack up and I feel like we're on firmer footing, here in the past. But it's a weird place for me. Like going to Luna Park - awesome fun but leaves you queasy.

Stu rubs a hand over his chin. 'How's your Dad?'

Four sips to get to this question. 'He's okay. Bit worse, but they're managing.'

'I see them a bit. Say G'day when I can, check in and that. They were always good to me.'

'Thanks, mate. Appreciate it.' I take another sip to get rid of the lump in my throat.

'I dunno. My folks go to church every Sunday,' he shrugs. 'Plenty of people believe in shit that's not real. Not hurting anyone. Just a few harmless traps in the bush, so what?'

So what? I think. *So what* is the thing you say when it's not your dad.

Three years ago. I'm legal now and I'm in this classroom that smells of sandstone and privilege, shitting myself. When the tutor asks us for introductions and I mention Tassie, I get the usual titters from kids who think the world ends at Parramatta Road.

But the history teacher frowns, 'Ah, the state of extinction,' and for a second, I'm cold. He knows, my heart thumps. He knows about Dad, which is ridiculous because obviously he doesn't know but it's amazing how the fear of being found out screws with your head.

So I go to ground. For weeks, I don't speak in tutes, then we have this lesson where he tells us about Risdon Cove, the massacre and all the indigenous men, women and kids gunned down. He gives me this raised eyebrow and for an awful second, I'm relieved because I get that his extinction reference wasn't about Dad or Tigers at all.

I still hate myself for that.

By the time I get to the traps, it's late afternoon and the bush is all purple khaki and shadows. This place of death. This place of murder. Like I said, open spaces aren't all created equal. In the morning I'm going to see if I can get an earlier flight. Tell Mum I've got to get back so I can finish an assignment. That first Bondi swim will clear my head.

Gravel crunches like bone under my boots. The first trap is empty. So is the second one.

I go to the third and stop. There's something inside and that's not unusual - sometimes he gets a stray Tassie devil or quoll that's wandered in by mistake. But for a second, just a single second, I'm hopeful. I want it so bad.

But it's just a roo, a delicate female.

Disappointment beads on me like sweat. I open the trap, jostle it a little to scare her into moving. Behind the wire, she watches me with these terrified currant-eyes and I wait, not moving, until she melts into the rustling scrub. So happy to be free.

At home, Dad's slumped on the couch watching the Demons v Bombers, one leg thrust out, the other folded. I jingle the keys and he looks, sits up with hope, muscles tensed for a moment where something is possible. 'Anything?'

'Nup. All empty.'

He grunts, slumps. The TV shouts with another goal to the Bombers and misery returns to my father's shoulders. Mum walks in with plates of curry, rich with spice and onions.

'Smells great, Mum. Ta.' I take one off her hands.

'Good on you, darl.' Grateful, always grateful.

'What's this muck?' Dad drops a fork load back onto the bowl and the lamb sticks in my throat like sadness.

'It's curry, Kev. You like this one.'

'Looks like shit.' He pushes it away and Mum gives me this look that reminds me of the little roo in the cage.

A decision clicks in me. My divided, four-chamber heart pumps away, blood going right to left, oxygen fuelled.

I swallow the meaty sauce. 'You know, Dad, when I was driving back, I think I saw something…'

They're both watching me now and I speak into the sadness until Dad bounds out of the chair to go get his exercise book.

'Thank you, love.' Mum takes my hand. The room exhales like a trap door has opened. 'Thank you.'

Christmas Lights
Jackie Woods

Michelle carried the ladder, which was not as heavy as Andrew had always made out, down the side path. She steadied it against the wall and climbed high enough to fasten the LED 'flying angel with trumpet' to the gutter.

She jiggled and budged, but the angel hung precariously, its wings obscuring the back of Santa's sleigh mid-flight to the chimney.

Bugger it, she thought. It's Christmas Eve. The lights will come down soon. It'll do.

Michelle stepped back down the ladder. She plugged the cord into the outside power point they'd had specially installed, flicked the switch to on and 'flying speed' to high. She could just make out the wings flashing vigorously up and down in the fading sunlight.

Michelle's neighbour Emma powered past, pushing her toddler in a stroller loaded with green bags.

'I didn't think you'd find room for another one,' Emma called out from the footpath.

'Always room for an angel!' Michelle said back, too brightly.

'Angel!' shouted the little girl, wiggling her legs and pointing. 'Angel fly!'

'Yes Gabby, the angel is flying,' said Michelle.

Emma pushed the stroller and excited child faster, disappeared through her front gate and up the next-door path. 'I'll keep the fire brigade on speed dial in case it all goes up in flames, ha ha.'

Michelle rolled her eyes behind the camellia.

The year they moved in, Sammy was an 18-month-old rocket with a saggy nappy and vegemite mouth. She and Andrew felt so smug for giving him his own room and a patch of grass–property owners! They had never thought of Christmas lights.

Then Sammy fell in love with a starburst on the next block. Those long evenings Andrew was working late, or pretending to, things at home could turn from bliss to screaming mess quicker than a heartbeat. Michelle would take him to watch the star work its silver and blue LED magic–little, bigger, biggest–and he would point and say 'Star! Star!' and the world would slow down for a blessed moment.

The next year, Andrew bought their own flashing gold star. They hung it in the centre of the porch, drank real champagne and toasted Christmases to come.

Michelle poured a strong gin and tonic in the kitchen and took it out to the footpath for a last look at her house before the sun was fully down and the parade of spectators arrived.

The gold Star Zero was in its place over the porch.

Attached to the front of the fence was the red and green Merry Christmas they'd bought next, light swooshing along the cursive letters as though the final text was going to be a surprise, like skywriting.

The candles with holly were on the front grill. They were as ugly as ever. Andrew had made a point of buying them from the cheap rack because wasn't it time she went back to work? They were on one income and Sammy was about to start school, for crying out loud.

The inflatable snowman taking up too much of the front yard was Sammy's choice. She'd questioned if snowmen were actually Christmassy but it was the year she had two miscarriages and finally gave up trying for another baby. If Sammy wanted the snowman that was fine. They called him Stumpy and she couldn't remember why. At least they wouldn't have to add a room, or move.

Michelle bought the glass birds glistening in the camellia–fairy wren, rosella, lorikeet, cockatoo–the year she got a new job and then a promotion five months later. Andrew said they were much less Christmassy than Stumpy, but they were expensive and handblown and she loved them.

The LED waving Santa–Flat Santa aka Hello Santa–was in his place on the front wall next to the window. His arm seemed to emerge from his pants and Michelle lived in hope someone would say, 'Is that a candy cane in Santa's pocket?' They never did.

The centrepiece, Santa in his sleigh with four reindeer stretching across the narrow width of the red tiled roof, was from the year Andrew found a text on her phone saying *Good night beautiful*, which she insisted was a wrong number but wasn't. The Santa sleigh and growing enthusiasm from neighbours got them into the Daily Telegraph's Top 10 Christmas Streets feature that year and she still had the framed clipping on the wall–*SANTA'S HELPERS: Michelle and Andrew with son Sam (12) light up their neighbourhood with Christmas cheer.*

The golden curtain of lights hanging from eaves to ground were a present from Andrew the year she found text messages on his phone. *Hi sexy!* [Headless torso in lace underwear]. He didn't pretend they were from a wrong number. Anyway, the name was right there–Megan Guitar Teacher. He was sorry, he'd made a terrible mistake and they changed guitar teachers for Sam without telling him why. The long, fine strings of lights formed a beautiful shining net, or cage.

No new Christmas decorations were added during their long year of marriage counselling.

The candy cane solar torches planted in the ground around Stumpy were from the year her mother said, 'You know, I would have left your father years ago if I'd had the guts. There are no prizes for being miserable.' What?

She had bought the plastic nativity scene (vintage) set up on the porch at a garage sale after Andrew announced Megan was six months pregnant and they were having a baby. It was only three months since he'd left the family home. Michelle asked if that made him Joseph or God, he said it made him sorry she couldn't be happy for anyone but herself.

Earlier this year, before leaving interstate for uni, Sam had given her a George Jensen gold heart on a red cord. It was only February but she'd hung it over the front window, which had always been Sam's room, where it had stayed.

Sam's gold heart was going to be the last new thing.

But the Facebook algorithm knew her too well. When the angel popped up in her feed at 2am she'd clicked and Apple-paid before taking a minute to consider that she could admire Christmas bling without putting it on the front of her house.

As she looked at the angel, dangling from the corner eaves, wings flapping, she knew it wasn't the only thing tipping her display from charming to eccentric, but it didn't help.

Michelle sat in her chair on the porch, behind the golden curtain, the glow of lights getting brighter as the sun went down.

Christmas Eve was always the buzziest night for light-viewing–kids wired and parents desperate to channel that Santa energy.

'Can you see Santa? He's coming when you're asleep tonight!' 'Max, look at the reindeers on the roof! There's Rudolph and Dancer and Prancer and what are the others called?' 'Can we put some carrots out?' 'Can we get a snowman like that, Dad?' 'What colours can you see, Bubby? Red! Blue! Gold! Green! Pink! Pretty!' 'Better get your sunglasses out for this place, babe.'

Emma sometimes appeared in her unadorned front yard on these warm nights, saying: 'The real estate agent never told us the street becomes a theme park in December!' or 'We need traffic control around here at Christmas!' or 'I just can't justify using so much electricity!' But there was no sign of her tonight.

Michelle's phone pinged.

Sure you won't join us for lunch tomorrow? We've got a place for you [clinking glasses emoji].

It was Julie, who she didn't think of as a best friend until this past year when she had leaned into Michelle's new status as single empty-nester, when so many others had leaned out.

Thankyou lovely but I'm all sorted [Smiley, folded hands, kiss].

Sam was spending Christmas with Andrew and Megan and his little half-sister. They'd invited him down the coast. He'd asked would she mind and she'd said of course not.

December 25 was just another day after all and Michelle took the chance to sign up for Self Care Christmas™, which she'd heard about on a podcast. 'I take care of *me!*' the American host had enthused to gasps and applause of an unseen audience. 'I know that I won't ever give up on *me*. I will never abandon me. The one person I need is *right here!*'

'The one person I need is right here,' Michelle said to herself in the bathroom mirror as she cleansed, moisturised, tied back her long hair. She pictured herself waking fresh in the morning, enthusiastically tackling the schedule sitting in her inbox, subject line: *Nurture yourself to wholeness and joy this Christmas!*

But Michelle didn't wake fresh, even though she hadn't had that many gin and tonics on the porch. She was already behind schedule when she set the timer for the first activity: '30 minutes journaling'.

She made a coffee, and another. The instructions said *don't think and let the first words in your mind flow to the page, clear any blockages, discover your true voice.* She stared at the blank page, changed her timer ringtone to 'chimes' then 'crystals' and was relieved when it finally went off. She crossed journaling off her list and '30 minute walk or jog' as well. No-one would know.

Next up was yoga. She rolled out her mat on the small back deck but sounds floating through the fence–furniture dragged over pavers, squeals of present-opening delight–were much too distracting.

She skipped ahead to 'festive bircher muesli' (soaked oats and chia with berries, not that festive) and then 'Present time. Slowly and lovingly unwrap your gifts to yourself'. She hadn't bothered wrapping her presents to herself because she knew what they were–yellow sandals with silver buckles, a book about old growth forests from her work Secret Santa (she suspected it was a review copy sent to the office) and a giant Toblerone she had bought for Sam but switched to her own pile yesterday.

She put the sandals on and flicked through the book. Those are some impressive pictures of trees she said to herself, trying to feel more grateful. Tall. Old. Mossy.

She postponed 'creative time' (how could she sketch in the garden with all that noise?) and 'healthy feast' because she knew what the schedule wanted her to cook and it was not a feast.

Laughter and wafts of baked ham pushed through the fence and followed Michelle to her bedroom where she put her headphone on, lay on the bed, pulled up the covers and opened the Toblerone.

When the noise next door finally died down and afternoon faded to dusk Michelle got up, poured a gin and tonic, opened the front door and walked out to her chair on the porch.

She started when she saw Emma sitting there while little Gabby played with the nativity set. Emma jumped up, red-eyed.

'I'm sorry, it was so quiet here. I thought you were having Christmas out.'

'Stay there, I'll get another chair. Are you ok?'

'Oh all good, thanks,' Emma hovered, unsure whether to sit back down. 'Gabby stop that, be gentle.'

The child picked up each piece of the nativity set and examined it, banged it against the concrete lip of the porch, then put it back. Lamb - bang bang bang. Mary - bang bang.

'It's ok it's just plastic,' said Michelle, but the two women winced as the child banged baby Jesus in his manger against the concrete. 'Sounds like you had a big day?'

Emma sighed and sat. 'It's exhausting. Dom's family is so big and loud and they expect the works for Christmas lunch. They bring mountains of plastic crap for Gabby even though I try to set limits. It's too much. His parents are still there, I just had to escape for a moment.'

'Can I get you a G and T?'

'No, I've still got the dishes. Actually yes, maybe I will if you don't mind?'

Michelle went into the kitchen, realising it was the longest conversation she'd ever had with her neighbour. The family moved next door in June–Emma, who left the house each morning in a navy suit; her husband Dom with his odd hours and uniform, probably a nurse or ambo; and their fierce and enchanting two-year-old Gabby, whose tantrums alternately delighted and appalled Michelle through the fence. After initial introductions they'd settled into largely ignoring each other's presence out the front, a pattern only interrupted by the younger woman's disdain for the Christmas lights.

Michelle returned to the porch with a chair and another full glass.

They watched Gabby climb down the three front steps and into the garden, where she poked and patted Stumpy, hard.

'Did you see your family today?' asked Emma.

'Well I decided to try something new and have Christmas to myself this year.'

'Oh my god that sounds amazing!'

'Um yeah it was great, very relaxing.'

Dom stepped out of the front gate next door and did a double take when he spotted the women on the porch. 'Oh there you are,' he called out to Emma. 'I just came to see where you and Gab got to.'

'Excuse me a sec,' Emma said softly as she walked down to the fence. Hissed highlights from the couple's exchange floated up to the porch. 'No respect' 'I'm her mother' 'they're my parents' 'minute to myself' 'you're not the only one who's tired'. It was a familiar volley and Michelle closed her eyes and relaxed into the gin and oddly soothing backdrop of another couple's discord, smiling at the thought she could play either side convincingly. Her eyes shot open as Dom shouted 'Shit' and the timer for her light display ticked over, the house lighting up like a casino.

Emma's giggling broke the silence as their faces flashed green and red and gold. 'Gabby, see the crazy lights honey? Hang on. Gabby where are you Princess? She was just here a minute ago.'

The three adults peered into the small front yard, but the child wasn't there.

'Maybe she went back home?' said Emma, running up the neighbouring path.

Dom called up and down the street, 'Gabby, Gabriela. Where are you sweetie?'

'I'll see if she's gone inside,' said Michelle. She did a sweep of the short hall, glancing into each room. Not there.

Turning the lights off could help, she thought. What if she was there all the time and they just couldn't see her for all the flashing and carrying on? Michelle walked back out to porch, down the front steps and around to the side path, calling softly, 'Gabby? Gabby, are you down here love?'

There was no sign of the child, until she heard a small voice above. 'Angel fly!'

The girl was nearly at the top of the ladder she'd left against the wall yesterday. She was reaching for the angel's dangling, flashing wing.

Michelle froze. 'Come down now,' she said softly, wary of frightening her. She climbed a couple of rungs but the ladder wobbled and she stepped back down.

'Come down Gabby, we'll go out the front and look at the angel.'

But the girl was determined. She reached and grabbed the angel's wing, stepped off the ladder and hurtled towards Michelle, slowed only by the electrical cord catching on the down pipe.

The toddler landed hard against Michelle's chest, the force pushing her backwards. But she caught her! She caught her!

'Angel fly,' breathed Gabby, hot against her face, as the woman and child clung to each other.

Anxious calls came back into earshot: 'Gabby! Where are you? Come to Mummy.'

Holding the little girl tight, Michelle looked up to see the angel twisted out of shape and the Santa sleigh sliding off the roof. She switched the power off and the lights fell dead.

'I've got her! All good, she was just around the side,' Michelle called out, trying keep her voice steady. She lowered the girl to the ground and led her through the dark out to the footpath.

'Oh cheeky monkey,' Emma ran towards them, picking up her daughter. 'We didn't know where you were! Dom, Dom, she's here! Come see Nonna and Poppy and we'll have some ice cream.'

As her neighbours disappeared into the darkness, Michelle took the half-drunk gins inside and tipped them down the sink. She lay on the couch and tried to breathe, just breathe. But as she closed her eyes all she could see was the child's face rushing at her fast and hard. Michelle breathed and breathed until her breaths turned into gasps and gasps into sobs and she wept from a deep lake that might never empty.

Michelle woke up on Boxing Day, still on the couch, feeling fresh.

Before putting the kettle on, she went around the side of the house, climbed the ladder, disentangled the twisted angel from the gutter and lowered it to the ground. Since Andrew left she'd been getting someone in to install the Santa sleigh on the roof. But now Michelle climbed up on to the roof tiles and cut the rope attaching Rudolph to the chimney. The sleigh and reindeers fell to the ground.

She climbed back down and leaned the contorted angel and sleigh against the fence, mentally marking them 'for the tip'.

She made coffee and got to work on the front of the house. First, she wrapped the glass birds carefully, placing them in a box, put them in her bedroom cupboard. Then she took down Star Zero and the ugly candles, the Merry Christmas and Hello Santa, stacked them on the nature strip with a sign saying *In working order - Please take!* She pulled up the candy cane torches and cut the ties holding the curtain of golden lights in place under the eaves, folding the long strands into a plastic tub. She packed the nativity scene with its sheep and wise men, virgin mother and surprised father into a cardboard box. She deflated Stumpy and folded him into a Coles bag. All on to the pile.

She took Sam's golden heart from above the front window, took it inside and hung it from the picture rail above her bed.

She texted Julie: *Any leftovers?*

[Thumbs up.]

I'm on my way.

Michelle went inside and wrapped the old growth forests book for Julie. She put on her yellow sandals with a blue dress. As she walked out to her car, she could see Emma carrying the boxed nativity scene inside; the LED Merry Christmas propped up on her porch. They pretended not to see each other.

Roar

Justine Sless

'I'm poorly today, a bad tooth.' I lie to Mrs. Tanner.

'You don't look well mind Elsie.' Mrs. Tanner's words syphon from one corner of her mouth whilst the other corner clamps onto her Woodbine. She pulls the two fresh milk bottles closer to her padded blue dressing gown as if the bad tooth were contagious and the bottles will safeguard her.

'Tell Sharon I'll be in tomorrow.'

'Rightio pettle, look after yerself then.' Mrs. Tanner sniffs, looks past Elsie and scrutinizes the street.

I'm pleased Sharon didn't answer the door, she'd know just by looking at me that I'd lost another baby and then I'd lose my mettle and not be able to stop crying.

I'd love to stay home have a brew and nurse the ache, but I can't, I'm wearing my last pad so I'll have to get into town and buy some more.

I make my way up Villette Road. There's washing flapping down back alleys; sheets, shirts and a pair of grey keks big enough to cover ten arses. The radge man, tattoos of tigers etched onto the side of his shaved head, piercings crammed around the rim of each ear, is being pulled along by his two dogs down one lane. Their teeth are bared and three sets of eyes are glowering for a fight.

The libraries' just opening so I go in and use the toilet to check I'm not leaking. Clots as dark as liver squish against the pad and are cold against my fanny when I pull me keks back up. A stooped woman with gnarly hands at the borrowing desk smiles at me when I come out of the toilet. I want to ask if the Britannica would have an explanation for what's happening to my insides, but I know I'll just start blubbering if I try and talk and she'll pat my arm or worse suggest I see a doctor.

I did that once, the doctor looked at me over his glasses and told me I should be fretting about the son I have, not the ones I don't have.

Last time I was six weeks gone and then the blood came. This time it's four weeks. I didn't say anything to Billie, no point really. I just made out that I was going to work. In the early days I'd tell Billie, we'd get excited and think of names. One time when Mickey was little we told him that he was going to get a brother or sister. He cried when we said he'd be on his own a bit longer. It's been seven years now.

The bus is just pulling out from the stop when I get up to Ryhope road, so I keep walking, the cramps shuddering through me. My skirt's been rubbed more times than I can remember, I excuse the brown stain on tattie dust.

The big gates creak open at the Synagogue as I pass and a wifey comes out, her five children clumped around her. They never talk to you those Jews. Sometimes there's a big mob of them, nodding and talking quietly. The men wear long black coats all year and crazy round furry hats, ringlets bounce like springs over each ear and strings flutter from under their coats. They never look at anyone, not even when we pointed and called them names when we were kids. They always acted like they hadn't heard, so we got bored and stopped doing it.

The missus coming out of the Synagogue is wearing a wig, it's as stiff as a hat. Her little lads have round caps on their heads, ringlets and bits of string dangling from their clothes like their dad's. I wonder if the wifey sews the string onto the ends of their shirts and what they are for, what it's all for.

As she comes out of the gates, chalk white against her thick dark wig, one of her children drops a furry toy. The mam doesn't see it fall. It makes me nearly cry to bend over and pick it up.

'Here pet yer've dropped yer toy.'

The toy is between our hands, the mam's deep-set brown eyes don't quite look at mine.

It's like she wants to say something other than thank you. The six of them walk on, quietly. All of them dressed like they're on their way somewhere posh or to a funeral.

A fine mizzle dampens my face as I walk on. The leaves shuffle in the trees and the pain brings me to a standstill. I breath out and focus on the quietness of the school yard as I pass it, the weather vane zipping round against the grey sky on top of the St Peter's Church. When I pass the big terrace houses converted into medical rooms, I remember the time I spat out a pink minty drink after I had a filling at the dentist one time there when I was little. The silver glint of the filling like a snooping eye in my mouth.

The stone lions at the entrance of Mowbray park have turned dark grey from the drizzle and the screaking of the sea gulls' cuts through the noise of the buses swishing past. Two of the gulls swoop down, stamp their feet in a puddle and eye me off optimistically for scraps of food.

A fine sweat has broken on my brow from the pain. I grip the loops of the railings round the war memorial and stare up at The Winged Figure of Victory statue, she has a torch in one hand and a wreath in the other. She's looking out over the park, her job is to remember all of the dead men. There are poppies around the bottom of the statue, still there from November and still bright as fresh blood.

Be grand if there was someone looking out for all of the lasses round town, making sure that the supping of pints by sons and husbands doesn't use up all the rent money and slurred words don't turn into fists.

The pad is just a clag of blood around my arse and fanny now, the weight of it slowing me down.

I'm nearly crying by the time I get to shop. I ferret around my purse for all of the one and two pence pieces that I've collected from the jam jars on top of the fridge. The woman at the counter says,

'Take yer time pettle, take yer time.' I want to tell her that I've lost another bairn and that the pain is nothing compared to the sadness.

I cross over to the museum for the toilet. The hush inside the big glass doors and warmth is smashing.

I peel off my knickers and use wads of toilet paper to clean myself up as best I can. Clots splash into the water. The ache sits at the bottom of my guts. I put on a clean pad, then walk through the museum. Past the glass cabinets of butterfls, stilled forever by pins stuck through their wings. Past the rows of quartz all glistening purples and apricot shimmers.

I sit down on the long black seat in front of Wallace The Lion, the museum's oldest stuffed animal. His head is half turned, staring out at me through his glass case. He used to scare me when I was little, but today his eyes have got more life in them than I can keep going in my own belly.

I shiver and think about how good it would be to snuggle up to his mane or have it always sewn onto a coat. When he was alive he must have had a right swagger on him, padding through the jungle, tearing up things to eat and roaring at the zebras.

Globules of blood bubble out of me. Maybe it's a teeny tiny arm, or maybe it's the babies face oozing, or maybe it's the baby's heart, pulsing one last time.

Career Girl

Emily Tosh

When Nettie stepped off the tram that Friday evening, she held a plain wrapped parcel tied with string against her shoulder as one might hold an infant. She walked briskly along the broad street before crossing into the lane where Mrs Forrester's tall terrace bookended a row of identical houses. High above, rain clouds clumped in a sunless sky, their ink blue colour matching the stain between the two fingers of Nettie's writing hand. In minutes she would be in her room pulling off hat and gloves, kicking off heels, wriggling out of garter and stockings, throwing off a skin tightening around her since morning. She adjusted her grip on the parcel, fingertips caressing the surface, and quickened her step almost whooping aloud.

It would not do to enter the house without visiting the parlour to greet Mrs Forrester. Widowed, her only son lost in the war, the old woman relished the exchange of a few words with her boarder. Nettie knocked, pausing a moment, before pushing the door open just enough to lean through with her head. She inhaled the stuffy air. A fire burned in the hearth and Mrs Forrester sat deep in an armchair knitting beneath the glow of a table lamp. The room had not been altered in thirty years, save for the addition of a chunky wood radio that sat mostly silent, Mrs Forrester's taste culling broadcasts to a slim number.

'Good evening, Mrs Forrester.'

The old woman lifted eyes to peer at Nettie over the rim of spectacles perched on the end of her nose. 'Oh, Nettie dear, you're home. Was it a busy day?' Her fingers, meanwhile, continued to deftly work the wool.

'It was rather hectic. Cataloguing in the morning and the afternoon on loans and returns.'

'Well, I expect you're hungry. There's a pot of soup on the stove and bread on the table.'

'Thank you, Mrs Forrester, but I ate a late lunch and have letters to write before I turn in.' Nettie smiled her gratitude, keeping the parcel out of sight behind the door, for the kindly Mrs Forrester could also be curious.

'Suit yourself, dear, but a career girl like you needs her strength.'

'Really, I'm not hungry. Good night, Mrs Forrester.'

'Very well, dear. Good night.'

Released, Nettie hurried up the stairs to her room. Hugging the parcel under one arm, she took the key from her handbag and unlocked the door, making sure to relock it on the other side. The darkness was relieved by pale streetlight seeping through the window and, for now, Nettie preferred it that way. She dropped her handbag to the floor then crossed to the bed where she placed the parcel on top of the linen counterpane. It lay there like an offering on an altar, and she stood before it excited and awed. Hastily, she threw off her bindings - coat, gloves, hat, dress, and undergarments - leaving them in a pile. Standing naked at last, her flesh goose bumped and her nipples puckered. There, in the privacy longed for all day, she trembled.

Nettie suppressed her impatience, determined not to bow to haste, and instead went about her preparations in a deliberate fashion. She drew the curtains, switched on the ceiling light, and removed a suitcase from inside a huge, oval mirrored wardrobe. It seemed a menacing piece of furniture to Nettie, its cyclopean eye reflecting what she mostly loathed to see. Asking Mrs Forrester to replace the wardrobe with another had seemed too irrational to seriously consider. And so, for the moment, Nettie fixed her eyes on the suitcase she carried to the bed and placed beside the parcel.

Clicking the suitcase locks, she lifted the lid and began removing the garments, draping each item neatly over the footboard of the single bed. When finished, she turned to the parcel, her final purchase. She untied the string and tore off the paper revealing a box bearing the maker's brand. Delight spilled out of Nettie in a light chuckle. Opening the box, she reached in and lifted the shoes, holding them up before her–brown and tan with that new leather smell. The decorative stitching in a wing pattern on top was, in Nettie's opinion, the feature that made these Oxfords classy. They were lace-ups, flat heeled, comfortable and expensive, an extravagance Nettie was unwilling to forgo. In fact, over the past month, she had put a sizable dint in her savings. It was worth every penny to feel herself come to life like the proverbial desert after rain.

It was time to dress, a prelude to tomorrow night's gathering, and in the cold of the room the thought thrilled and flushed Nettie with heat. She began with singlet, drawers and socks. Next, she pulled on a white cotton shirt fastening the buttons to the collar. The sleeve edges were buttonless and these she pinched together by inserting silver cufflinks. In preference to a belt, she attached braces to brown tweed trousers a touch loose around the waist. She looped a burgundy silk tie around the collar of her shirt, wove a knot at the neck letting the ends hang down to her waist. Finally, she slipped on and laced up her Oxfords then completed the ensemble with a wide lapelled jacket matching her trousers. Nettie looked down at herself as she ran her hands over her body stroking the different fabrics marvelling at her daring.

Mirrors were a source of discomfort for Nettie, and she often avoided them. When examining herself, she saw incoherence. Outwardly, she possessed fine individual traits though, in combination, they somehow missed beauty's mark. Perhaps it was the aquiline nose beneath winter brown eyes or the angular jawline or a certain lack of grace in her bearing. Inwardly, she strained against expectations of femininity. Women's attire made Nettie feel strangled, ridiculous and self-conscious. For as long as she could remember, inside and outside were as immiscible as oil and water. Now, though, she moved eagerly to stand before the wardrobe and gazed into its silvery eye. 'Oh God,' she whispered.

Nettie stood blinking, hardly able to believe the transformation. A woman in a man's suit, legs planted slightly apart, stared back at her. She adjusted her tie. She turned a little this way and that, her eyes studying her twin. She gathered her auburn hair holding it back with one hand then slid the other inside her trouser pocket. She smiled and stood taller. This was not impersonation, this was discovery. Nettie was meeting her true self for the first time, and she was magnificent. Outside, in the night, a single gust of wind stirred the air and the first raindrops began to fall.

In her time at university, first as student and later as employee, Nettie had read all she could to understand her wrong-headedness. There were names for her particular inclination, medical terms befitting an unnatural specimen needing to be treated and cured rather than loved. There were other names too, like those spat from her father's tight, thin-lipped mouth with the same violent disgust of one having swallowed a blowfly. Names that twisted her stomach, forcing her to stoop and void its sour liquid contents onto her mother's favourite rug.

It happened several years earlier, on a sweltering day, the hottest of that summer. Nettie was home on the farm after completing her time at boarding school. She had passed all subjects, including her least favourite–Latin–with honours and been offered a bursary to study at university. All she needed was her father's consent which he had refused, 'There's no need. You'll marry one day and have children.' By mid-afternoon, clouds had evaporated from the sky, distances were made hazy by the heat and the incessant sizzle of cicadas pitched higher in air. The obligations of the morning were behind Nettie and she was free to spend time at the river. It was a good place to escape the house though, given the chance, she would have gone further.

The river, wide as one of her father's wheat fields, almost touched the farm's northern boundary as it wound across the land like a plump vein. The local children called it The Pool, and all summer they giggled, squealed and splashed, leaping into the cool water from ropes tied to tree branches. As a child Nettie joined in, stripping down to her shift before swinging out to plunge in legs first. She stopped all that some time ago. Upstream was a quiet, shaded place where she could stretch out on a smooth rock and read.

Wearing a brimmed hat and clutching the drawstring of a cloth bag, Nettie started up the farm's dirt road. The gravel crunched beneath her feet and before long her ankle boots were covered in dust. She was still brooding about events during the lunchtime meal. She had thought it a good time to again raise the subject of the bursary, but managed to say very little before her father cut in with a decree she knew was final. Her mother, a slender plank of a woman, maintained a wooden silence and her older brother continued to eat not looking in her direction, sulky at his exclusion from military service. The memory made her kick at a stone and then another, the sudden movement momentarily dispersing the circling flies.

Partway along the road, Nettie turned onto a track offering a shorter path to the river. Sweat traced lines down her spine with the lightness of fingertips and she scratched where it itched. It wasn't just the temperature making her uncomfortable. Her day dress seemed all wrong. It tied at the back in a foolish bow and caught on the dry brush where the track narrowed. She was lost in thoughts of stealing a pair of her brother's overalls when the river came into view behind a stand of peeling gums. Nettie closed her eyes and let out a long breath, glad she could finally shelter from the brutal day.

When Nettie came out of the trees, she stood on the piece of rocky bank she had claimed as her own. Ahead, the river moved on a slow current. She stepped her way to the edge then removed her boots and hitched up her dress to sit. In this shallower part of the river, light and shadow mottled the water green and gold. Nettie lowered her feet through the surface, felt the cool rise, shuddered once and relaxed.

This was an ancient place, Nettie could feel it, and she imagined long ago people fishing the waters where her feet now soaked. She leaned back on her hands and closed her eyes, listening to the call of birds. She knew the magpie, bellbird, whipbird, and was concentrating on a warble, unable to name its owner, when a sound from behind made her start and turn. 'Hello Nettie,' called a voice she had not heard for many months. Nettie, who suddenly felt the flutter of wings inside her chest, raised and dropped her hand giving a faint wave. Spellbound, she kept her eyes on the girl walking towards her and soon found herself staring up at the face of Edith Moran. It was impossible to speak and it was impossible to look away. Nettie had grown stiff with awkwardness.

'Your brother said you had a spot down this way.' Edith looked around, 'It's pretty.' She promptly sat and in no time her bare feet paddled lazily in the water beside Nettie's. When she again turned her face towards Nettie, they were so close Nettie could see the green and gold flecks in Edith's hazel eyes, as inviting as the river water, and she strained against their tow to gaze instead at the smooth liquid flow before her.

'What do you do here by yourself?' Edith asked.

Nettie battled her unwilling tongue. Normally so good with words, she could squeeze out no more than one. 'Read,' came her clipped reply. The red rose in her cheeks and she sat hunched under her hat staring ahead.

'Ah, that makes sense. He calls you The Bookworm.'

Nettie knew her brother to be a boorish oaf, but mocking her to friends and neighbours was a new low. It spiked her anger and she spun on Edith only to be instantly disarmed by her smile.

'I like it,' Edith laughed and nudged Nettie with her shoulder. 'The Bookworm,' she repeated and laughed a little louder. And Nettie suddenly laughed out loud too, their sounds merging and ringing in this quiet place. The tense knot at Nettie's core loosened, and she grew acutely aware of Edith's arm resting against her own.

It was soon clear Edith enjoyed talking, and she shifted the conversation from trivial to serious with the randomness of lightning strikes - her mother's best rabbit pie recipe, the town boys off fighting the war, Jap subs in Sydney Harbour, the brown snake inside the Catholic church outhouse. Nettie spoke less, finding pleasure in listening to Edith's voice and secretly studying the landscape of her face. For a moment, she considered asking about her brother's recent visits to the Moran farm before judging it an intrusion. They pulled their prune-skinned feet from the water. Nettie reached into her bag for an apple and passed it to Edith feeling a secret spark at the brief touch of fingers. She watched Edith's soft mouth sink into the apple's flesh, heard the crunch and felt again that spark when she took the apple from Edith's hand. In tacit agreement, each bite overlapped the one before, the apple going back and forth until only the hard, seeded centre remained.

The sun blazed lower from the west signalling it was time to go home. In a few hours, there would be darkness and relief from its hectoring heat. The two girls walked the short distance back to the track and there they lingered, drawing out a little more of the afternoon. 'Could I meet you here again?' asked Edith softly, some hesitation in her voice.

Nettie's answer needed no thought. 'Yes, I want that.'

The words released something between them so that Edith moved closer placing her arms over Nettie's shoulders to hold her in an embrace. Nettie's response was instant. Her hands went to Edith's waist and pulled her tighter. They stood pressed together, senses alive to every touch, every movement, and every pounding beat of their hearts. Abruptly, Edith broke free, put her lips to Nettie's then turned and ran in the direction of her farm. Nettie's eyes stayed on her as she moved further away. When Edith reached a bend in the track, she stopped and whirled round, waved her arm and called, 'See you soon, Bookworm!' Seconds later, she was lost from sight and Nettie began walking homeward, her mind on that first kiss. Brief and closed-mouthed, it would always be the most perfect moment of her life.

Nettie arrived home humming, the day's frustrations forgotten. She did not notice her father's truck by the side of the house, a sign he was home early. As she set foot on the verandah, the screen door shot open and slammed into the sandstone wall leaving a chip. Out charged her brother, red face snarling and snorting with fury. 'I wish you were dead!' he roared, knocking her away as he headed to the fields. The force sent Nettie staggering backwards off the verandah to fall onto flat, hard earth. She landed on her back with a grunt, the skirt of her dress twisted and raised over her thighs. Shaken and confused, she struggled to her feet, tugged down her dress and rubbed the places where it was beginning to hurt. Her hat and bag lay in the dirt nearby and she winced in moving to retrieve them. None of it made sense. The tread of boards drew her eyes back to the house. Her father stood pinch-browed at the open door. 'Front room, now,' he ordered.

The front room showcased her father's success and her mother's astute choice in matrimony. It was the best room in the house where guests were entertained and her father sometimes conducted farm business. One morning each week was dedicated to its thorough dusting and polishing by her fastidious mother. Nettie stood at the threshold, her back sore. Fear, now greater than puzzlement, set her heart to a faster pace.

Before the mantlepiece stood her father, rigid and cold like one of its carved marble columns. He beckoned her forward, pointing with his finger to the centre of the room. Nettie obeyed, advancing slowly. Although the room lay on the afternoon shaded side of the house, it had absorbed enough heat to make sweat rise on the brow. Nettie noticed the sleeves of her father's shirt rolled up above the elbows exposing thick, hair covered forearms. His hands lay by his side, clenched into fists. She knew her father to be stern and absolute, not violent. Today, for the first time, the threat of his violence hung in the room.

The confrontation was explosive and one-sided. Nettie suddenly found herself at the centre of a maelstrom of accusations and abuse. She had been seen by her brother with Edith. In a voice bloated with anger, her father called her wicked, shameless, a pervert intent on ruining her brother's future. He wielded words like a club, without once touching his daughter.

At one point, her mother materialised and Nettie saw her standing off to the side wearing an apron. Amid the terror of the moment, Nettie's mind latched onto the incongruity of her mother's housemaid appearance in the fancy room and she began to laugh–a desperate, wild laugh that grew until broken by a rib-aching hiccup. Looking across at her mother, Nettie saw her lips constrict into a moue of revulsion. She was a woman who habitually contained her thoughts, rarely offering an opinion beyond matters of household management, and so her terse verdict delivered an unexpected sting. 'It's a dirty thing, Nettie. Dirty!'

'Please, I don't understand,' Nettie cried.

Her father, as usual, had the last say. 'Tomorrow morning you leave this house.' In response, Nettie's stomach heaved, forcing the acidic remains of the apple to surge up into her throat and out of her mouth in a spray of vomit.

Nettie felt the pain of that time less these days, yet it was her lot to live always with a part of it pressing against her heart. Some nights, the events entered her mind during sleep, haunting her dreams, jolting her awake before leaving behind the sediment of a heavy mood. The nightmares stoked the fire of her fear, making her more conscious of holding people like Mrs Forrester at arm's-length. Nettie lived quietly, discreetly, keeping company with other career girls at private parties, like the one scheduled next evening at the residence of a friend. Careful to get away without Mrs Forrester scrutinising her behaviour too closely, she had long ago hit on the excuse of an overnight visit with a married cousin. Tomorrow, there would be few questions when she left carrying her suitcase.

The rain lost its restraint falling hard and full, quickly saturating the city. Gutters filled, overflowed and sloshed down to the pavement below. Nettie remained in front of the mirror consumed by the handsome vision. It wasn't simply that the clothes suited her, it was that they changed something fundamental in her. They made her feel right. Oh, what an entrance she would make! And this time, when the gramophone played, she would ask someone to dance. The smile stretched wider across her face as she took a last look at her reflection. Then, heaving a sigh, she tore herself away, going to stand by the bed. Nettie looked down at the empty suitcase, reached up to loosen her tie and began to undress.

Christmas Charades
Andrea Barton

Christmas Day, 1984. Mum burned the turkey, I got Wham!'s *Make It Big*, and Uncle Rupert hit his head and died. Only in his fifties, Rupert seemed ancient to my 15-year-old self, but now I've passed the half century mark, it feels positively youthful.

Rupert's demise was pretty much as gruesome as it gets – he bled out, right there on the hearth in front of us. We tried to help, of course we did, but nothing worked. The coroner declared it an accident, but I always suspected there was more to it.

On that stinking hot day–Australian Christmases are nothing like the snow-filled wonderlands on gift cards–a pedestal fan stirred the warm air, barely cooling my sweaty limbs. Ten of us sat down for lunch: Grandma, Mum, Dad, Jake and Amanda (that's me), plus Rupert's gang of five. We stuffed ourselves to the brim with prawn cocktails, turkey, roast veggies, plum pudding, pavlova and all the trappings.

Mum cut the burnt bits off the turkey, and we all acknowledged it to be the tenderest bird of all time. She'd outdone herself, not only in the kitchen, but in every detail from the bejewelled artificial tree to the fancy crackers with jokes that actually made us laugh: *Why couldn't the skeleton go to the Christmas party? He had no body to go with.*

We all got into the spirit of the day, not to mention the spirits Mum handed around so liberally. My older cousin, Lara, winked at me when the adults weren't watching and slipped a nip of vodka into my orange juice. I thought she was pretty damn cool. Even 13-year-old Jake didn't object to wearing his paper crown. All in all, we were having a jolly good time.

We moved to the living room to open presents. The adults and cousins commandeered the lounge, armchairs and a few dining chairs. Only Jake and I sat on the floor. Our cousins had told Aunt Evelyn to buy me the Wham! album–on vinyl. What a thrill to be so trendy. These days it's a collector's item. Straight away, I set the record player going, and we all warbled away to 'Careless Whisper'.

Soon it was time for our traditional game of charades. The cousins hooted with laughter at Dad's hip thrusts and panting as he enacted 'She'll Be Coming 'Round the Mountain'.

Mum blushed and told him to behave.

Grandma shouted, 'Fucking…screwing…orgasm…' before Aunt Evelyn finally guessed the correct word.

I pretended to laugh along with the others but inwardly cringed at all this talk of sex. I couldn't wait for Dad's turn to be over.

Then Rupert was up. We all loved Rupert. Round-jowled and balding, at the peak of his accounting career, he ran his own company and sat on various boards. Power can go to a man's head, but not Rupert, at least, that's what everybody said. He found time to attend family gatherings, offered sage advice on any topic and always had a story to tell. Some might call it one-upmanship, but that would be uncharitable. Sure, he liked the sound of his own voice, but don't we all?

Rupert stood in front of the fireplace, tall and portly, reading his clue on a scrap of paper. We didn't have a fire, the sweltering heat put a stop to that, so Mum had placed a brass cauldron filled with pinecones in the grate. She'd adorned the mantlepiece with a eucalyptus garland, a touch of bush that scented the entire room and made a cheery backdrop.

I was on Rupert's team, so I studied him closely. He cut an imposing figure in his pumpkin-orange shirt–more Halloween than Christmas, but let's not quibble. Beer, wine and several potent cocktails made him sway on his feet. I inched behind the marble coffee table to keep out of his way.

He put his hands together, palms up, then held up four fingers.

'Book…four words,' I shouted in unison with Mum and the two cousins on my team.

Rupert nodded vigorously, held up one finger, then pinched his thumb and forefinger together.

We all yelled, 'First word…short word…the.'

He nodded again. Held up two fingers, stumbled, righted himself, then held his hand low to the ground.

'Second word, short,' Mum guessed.

Rupert shook his head.

'Tiny,' I said.

Another shake.

'Little,' my cousin suggested.

Rupert pointed at her, grinning wildly. He held up three fingers, then made fists with his hands, jerking them up and down.

'Third word. Hitting…banging…' Mum offered.

That wasn't it. Rupert straightened his back and jolted his hands some more.

'Drumming,' I said. 'The Little Drumming—'

'*The Little Drummer Boy*,' my cousin guessed.

Rupert gesticulated wildly, showing four fingers and pointing at me.

'*The Little Drummer Girl*?' I asked.

'Yes,' he whooped, dancing a little jig.

'Steady on,' Aunt Evelyn said as he staged an uninhibited butt wiggle. She wiped the corner of her eye and smoothed her foundation. Her makeup was always stage-worthy, unlike Mum, who preferred the natural look and didn't own a single wand of mascara.

As Rupert finished his performance, his foot caught on the hearth rug. He staggered, laughing at his clumsiness.

'Watch it, Dad,' Lara warned.

Too late. Rupert overcorrected and toppled forward. We watched, open-mouthed, too slow to reach out and help. His chortle broke off when his head hit the coffee table. The crack of bone on marble silenced the room. Rupert fell to the floor then rolled over, clutching his forehead.

No one moved. The fan hummed, rustling the discarded wrapping paper collected in a clothes basket. George Michael crooned on. Blood spilled from Rupert's head onto the green carpet. Red on green, merry bloody Christmas!

My aunt ran to him, crying, 'Call an ambulance'.

Already up, Mum raced to the phone. Dad took off his t-shirt, folded it over three times and held it to Rupert's wound.

Rupert looked at him and smiled. 'She'll be right, mate.'

'Sit him up,' Grandma instructed. 'Keep the blood away from his head.'

The cousins hurried to Rupert's side and helped Dad pull him upright. My brother Jake crept over to me, and we huddled together, watching the grisly scene.

By the time the ambulance arrived, Rupert's pulse was weak. He flickered in and out of consciousness. They rushed him to hospital.

Two hours later, he was declared dead.

The rest of the day was a bust.

I credit Uncle Rupert with sparking my interest in medicine. A few weeks after his death, I overheard Mum and Dad discussing the coroner's report. My childhood bedroom was right next to the kitchen and the heating vent that normally drove me barmy for carrying all the sound, made for eavesdropping heaven. Curiosity overcame me, and I listened in.

'Exsanguination,' Mum read. What a magical word for something that's nothing short of gruesome. We never did get the blood out of the carpet. Mum and Dad had it replaced.

Mum read all the autopsy's technical details. It boiled down to this: alcohol, alongside blood-thinning Warfarin prescribed for the stroke he'd suffered earlier that year, proved his undoing. Ever since, I've been intrigued by the power of drugs–recreational and prescription.

While the coroner ruled the death accidental, he also raised a question over the level of anticoagulant in Rupert's blood and suggested the cranberry cocktails Rupert drank that day might have potentiated–another glorious word–the effect of the medicine. Apparently, clinical trials had failed to prove the cranberry-Warfarin interaction, but anecdotal evidence was strong.

As my parents discussed this new information, I replayed that fatal Christmas day.

Truth be told, I was in a foul mood before our guests arrived. I'd argued with Mum about staying overnight at my boyfriend's house on New Year's Eve. Ridiculous! Yes, he was seventeen, two years older than me– I was the envy of all my girlfriends–but we wouldn't be alone, his parents would be home. Regardless, Mum, supported by Dad, wouldn't let me go. So, when Rupert and his family arrived, I was sulking in my bedroom.

Mum called out in a singsong voice, 'They're here,' but I stayed put.

Through the heating vent, I heard Aunt Evelyn. 'Where should I put all this?'

Evelyn, Mum's sister, always brought the pudding. She was a plum pudding expert, one of the few desserts I couldn't stand. Just the thought of all that dried fruit made my stomach curdle. After Mum showed her where to put the offending pudding, the champagne and everyone's presents, their volume dropped. Interest piqued, I pressed my ear so hard against the vent the metal patterned my skin.

'Are you doing okay?' Mum asked. 'Rupert hasn't done it again, has he? Here, let me check your face.'

Maybe I need to rewind. When I said everybody loved Rupert, I might have been whitewashing things a bit. My family had a gift for shoving things under the rug, like Jake did literally with his abhorred Brussel sprouts, or Mum figuratively with her empty gin bottles. You might say I learnt to present things the way they ought to be, an especially useful trick in relation to Christmas 1984.

But back to Evelyn. My pulse kicked up a notch when Mum said, 'You can stay with us if you want,' because whatever Rupert had done must have been bad if Evelyn was thinking about leaving him.

'I can't walk out,' Evelyn replied. 'What about the girls? I can't land all four of us on you.'

'Of course you can—'

But just then, the march of footsteps announced a new arrival, and Rupert boomed, 'Where's my favourite sister-in-law?'

Mum put on a cheery tone. 'Right here, in the kitchen as usual.' Louder, she called, 'Amanda, where are you? Our guests are here.' Her voice took on the edge that said I'd better not mess with her or there'd be *serious* consequences.

I hitched the neckline of my hideous red dress a little higher–Mum had insisted I wear something festive–and emerged from my room.

'Hi, Uncle Rupert, Aunt Evelyn.' I gave them each a dutiful kiss, noting Evelyn's Chanel perfume and dodging Rupert's enveloping hug.

He eyed me up and down. 'Look at you, the spitting image of your Aunt Evelyn.'

I couldn't see it myself. With my nose too big and my chin too small, I hardly mirrored Evelyn's Audrey Hepburn glamour, but my head swelled at the compliment.

Evelyn gestured to the door. 'The girls are in the living room with Jake.'

'Thanks, I'll go and say hi.' I tried to appear nonchalant while I studied her face. Her flawless foundation might have concealed a shiner. And all this time, I thought her face paint made her super chic.

As I was leaving, Mum asked, 'Cosmopolitan anyone?'

Evelyn put up her hand. 'Count me in.'

I gave a cheeky grin. 'Yes, please.'

Mum laughed. 'Nice try, Amanda. Maybe in three years' time.'

'I probably shouldn't.' Rupert shook his head slowly. 'Cranberry juice isn't a good mix with my meds.'

'It's Christmas.' Mum offered him a glass. 'How much harm can one do?' And here's the thing: she was a nurse, she'd have known.

'Oh, okay. Just one.' Rupert took the drink and downed half of it in one gulp.

In retrospect, I'm pretty sure Mum topped up his glass more than once.

But that wasn't all.

As I said, we had a jolly time at lunch, only perhaps it was more manic than jolly. Those cracker jokes were corny, but everyone laughed as though we were watching a Robin Williams movie. I didn't lie about the meal though; the turkey was a ripper. Rupert couldn't have asked for a better last meal.

My mood improved as I chugged my vodka and orange, so maybe I wasn't at my most observant, but I dimly recall Rupert taking his medication. At that age, I didn't take much interest in the old guy's tablets, but this simple act took on monumental significance in hindsight.

Afterwards, I couldn't help wondering whether somehow, someone slipped him an extra dose. I do remember this much–he asked Evelyn to give him his pillbox from her handbag.

Now that I'm a doctor, I'm aware that Warfarin tablets are colour-coded to help patients take the correct dose. I've scoured my murky memories over and over to picture what Rupert took that day. Would he have noticed if Evelyn upped his dose?

Did he really ask her, 'Are you sure this is the right amount?'

Did she really shrug and say, 'You're the one who manages all that'?

Because really, how hard would it have been for her to double his dose? A battered woman could almost be forgiven for doing such a thing.

I do know the pills were white. They looked innocuous, smaller than a regular painkiller. And the white Warfarin? They're the strongest. Most people couldn't take more than one. And he took two. I'm certain about that.

The coroner had suspicions, but not enough to take it any further.

Life went on. Well, not for Rupert. He'd been prepped like a turkey to the slaughter.

Christmas Day, 2021. Mum broke her silence, I had Covid, and Uncle Rupert returned to haunt me. I never used to believe in ghosts, but now I'm not so sure.

I spent this fraught day in isolation, hunkered down in my bedroom away from the rest of my family, who'd somehow escaped the virus. My husband, Tony, had been relegated to the couch in the living room, so I celebrated alone in my bed with its well-worn linen sheets. Luckily, my bedroom walls gave me plenty to look at: photos of my family and images of Australian flowers–banksias, proteas and wattles. The window overlooked the street, and I watched the neighbours drive off in their gaudy Christmas threads, most likely on their way to visit family they only connected with once a year.

Grandma had passed on and, these days, Mum and Evelyn's families celebrated independently, so with us in quarantine, Mum and Dad had Christmas at my brother Jake's house.

After they'd finished main course, Jake video-called to say hello. I couldn't hear him clearly with all the chatter and music blasting in the background–Elton John and Ed Sheeran's 'Merry Christmas'–but he bragged about the turkey, ham and stuffing with pine nuts. Normally, I'd have been jealous of such a spread, only Covid had stolen my ability to taste, so there wasn't much point. Kudos to Jake and his wife, Daisy; they'd done a stellar job making the place look celebratory. As an interior designer, Daisy loved nothing more than decorating for the holidays. The table centrepiece, crackers and napkins matched the room décor–soft pinks, whites and silver, not a crimson or green in sight.

Jake gave me motion sickness as he passed his phone around for me to say hi to each person. We didn't meet often during the year, so, like every Christmas, I gushed over how much his boys had grown. But what startled me the most was Mum's deterioration. I visited her every week or two, so I'm not sure why it struck me so hard. Maybe it was due to the interference on the line, the pixilated video, or the onset of a fever. In any case, her complexion seemed papery, her gaze a little vague. For the first time, I saw her as an old woman, fragile enough for a gentle breeze to knock her off her feet.

'Evelyn,' Mum said. 'Lovely to see you.'

My breath caught. 'It's not Evelyn, Mum, it's Amanda.' She'd been increasingly confused recently, but she'd always recognised me before. It must have been the distortion on the screen.

Mum obviously didn't hear me because she said, 'Evie, I'm glad you called. I've been thinking of you.'

'Mum, I—'

'Every Christmas I remember Rupert. We need to talk about it before it's too late.'

The skin prickled on the back of my neck. 'Mum, stop. It's me, Amanda.'

'Amanda?' She adjusted the phone, and a brittle tinkle of laughter rang out. 'Oh, of course it is. You look just like my sister, do you know that?'

'Yes, Mum.' She told me every time she saw me.

'How are you, love? I've been so worried about you with that dreadful virus.'

'Not too bad. Can't taste or smell anything, which takes all the fun out of food, and I'm overheating.' My temperature had spiked since Mum came on the phone, and I seemed to be having trouble breathing.

'Well, take care of yourself. I was just saying to Evie that we really need to discuss Rupert.'

'Rupert? Mum, he died thirty-seven years ago. Don't you remember?'

Mum sniffed. 'That's as may be, but we can't let this go on.'

My chest felt tight. I couldn't suck enough oxygen. I'd suffered asthma as a child, but those mild attacks had nothing on this. 'Mum, I have to go. I need to take another tablet.'

'Tablets were part of the problem. That's why I need to speak to Evie, but you...Amanda...it wasn't your fault. You couldn't possibly have known.'

'Mum, what are you talking about? I never—'

'I didn't bring you up to shy away from the truth.'

Who was she kidding? We were experts at charades. Everyone knew she enjoyed her gin a bit too much, but the word alcoholic never crossed our lips. I looked out the window and admired my blood red roses. So festive. 'Mum, I have to go. Say goodbye to Jake for me.'

I hung up before she could speak any more nonsense and tossed my phone on the dresser. Why was she unpicking our carefully embroidered past?

My head pounded, so I washed down some paracetamol with water. I pulled the sheets straight and sank into bed. Beads of perspiration formed on my forehead. Outside, it was thirty-two degrees in the shade, but usually, our house remained cool. 'Buy a solid brick house if you can afford it,' Dad had advised during our search for a family home. 'Weatherboards might look pretty, but they don't offer the same insulation.' He was right. But today, I was sweltering, a sweaty blob in a lake of fire. Covid was a nasty beast. I reached for the remote control and turned on the air-conditioner.

My medical experience proved that rest was a powerful cure, so I closed my eyes and tried to will myself to sleep.

Within minutes, the blasting cold air puckered my arms into goosebumps. I turned it off and huddled under the bedclothes. To no avail. Shivering uncontrollably, I curled into a ball and hugged my knees to my chest. If I worsened, I'd have to call my husband, but I hoped I could ride it out.

I must have fallen into an uneasy sleep because nightmares warped my mind to fix on Uncle Rupert. We stood in Mum's kitchen, carving an enormous pumpkin. I detested Halloween, just like I hated horror movies. I couldn't understand why people enjoyed fear. Real life had enough terrors. Rupert had cut the lid off the pumpkin and scooped out the insides. Flesh and seeds strung together by orange veins lay in a messy heap on the counter. I hacked eyes into the fruit–yes, pumpkin's a fruit, not a vegetable–and Rupert screamed.

I turned to face him in slow motion. He loomed over me, blood streaming from his eyes.

'Oh God, I'm so sorry.'

He gave a lecherous smile. 'You can make it up to me.'

Still grinning, he grabbed at me, but I pulled away, shocked by the blood, horrified by his groping hands.

'Hold me, just for a moment.' His wheedling tone put my every cell on guard.

'No. Stop it! I'll tell Mum.'

He leered at me, laughing. 'Tell her what? It's only a cuddle. There's nothing wrong with that. What's the matter with you?'

Vomit rose in my chest. I made for the bathroom, but pumpkin vines bound my ankles. Rupert's lusty eyes bored into me. His arms wrapped around me, forcing my face into his chest. I couldn't breathe, smothered by his denim shirt. The stench of garlic seeping through his pores made me gag.

Animal instinct jerked up my knee. It tore through the vines, straight for the balls.

Then I fled.

I pushed through fields of barley that clawed my legs. A snake rose between the fronds, ready to strike, fresh blood dripping from its fangs. I turned left. Another menacing serpent. Behind me, another.

Surrounded, I slipped into a different dimension.

I tumbled onto mudflats that swallowed my shoes and left me barefoot. A giant wave approached. I tried to wade through the deep sludge, but my feet were stuck. The water thundered closer. I couldn't outrun it. Couldn't move.

This was it. I was going to drown.

Heart racing, I turned to face it.

I sucked air and dived deep. The break caught me, tossed me in a wash of the past. Cold, oh so cold.

I stopped struggling and drifted. Teeth chattering, I floated on the glacial liquid. Salt water stung my eyes.

Soaked, I dragged myself onto snow that bit my toes. Icicles stabbed the soles of my feet.

I climbed mountains of sand, baking under the sweltering sun, and swam across oceans of memories.

I clawed my way back to my parent's loungeroom, Christmas 1984.

We gathered around the fireplace, puppets to some unknown force. White-blue flames raged in the grate. A garland of thorns dripped blood on the mantlepiece. Uncle Rupert danced on the hearth rug, a man possessed, his features a ghostly pallor. Arms reaching, pawing, mauling.

Evelyn watched, grotesque lipstick marring her cheeks. Mum, beside her, wore a giant nurse's hat. She cradled a syringe of cranberry juice. I left marionette Jake alone on the floor and sat on the dining chair Rupert had vacated to execute his lethal charade. With that act, I became a grown up like the other cousins, not the second youngest, still a child.

'Book…four words.'

'First word…short word…the.'

'Second word, short.'

'Tiny.'

'Powerless.'

'Pounding…thumping…'

'Drumming. The Little Drumming—'

'*The Little Drummer Boy.*'

Rupert pointed at me, accusing. '*The Little Drummer Girl?*'

Raucous laughter. Drumming. Rupert leaned forward to hug me. Whispered in my ear. His fingers snaked beneath my skirt.

I froze. My heart turned to stone. I couldn't make a scene, not in front of everyone. Who'd believe me? I wasn't an adult; I was a tiny little drummer girl. Powerless.

He chased me round the living room. Mum waved her syringe. Evelyn wiped her lips, smearing cerise bruises across her face. The others sat, lifeless dummies.

'Enough,' I snapped. 'Sit!' A tantrum. I was a tiny child, so I acted like a child.

The drumroll started imperceptibly. Beats fast as a hummingbird's wings, thousands of strikes merged into one. The noise built as Rupert lowered into the seat, peaked as I pulled the chair away from him. Hilarious. More raucous laughter. Pa-rum pum pum pum.

Rupert teetered backwards, overcorrected and toppled forward, cutting his head on the pure white, razor-sharp marble table. Blood gushed. My God, the blood.

Time skewed. The drumming slowed, each beat further apart. Blood pulsed. Filled the room. I floated on blood, choked on it, couldn't breathe, gasping and spluttering, drowning in blood.

I thrashed and wheezed. Pulled my mouth free. My legs tangled in the bedsheets. I gulped air, battling free of my dream.

Where was I?

The house was deathly silent. My fever ran high as I choked on memories. Every painful moment replayed in technicolour detail. The blooms on the walls slowly came into focus.

What did I do that Christmas day? Did I make Uncle Rupert fall? Did I realise how catastrophic a fall could be?

It was a dream, nothing but a dream. I didn't kill Uncle Rupert.

I couldn't have known about the cranberries. Or the tablets, the overdose. I couldn't have known any of that. I was just a little girl. All I did was pull the chair out from under him.

I. Did. Not. Kill. Rupert. I didn't. It was a careless prank, an accident like Mum said, not murder. I'm a doctor. I swore an oath to preserve life. I didn't murder Rupert.

Did I?

Christmas Day, 1984. Mum and Aunt Evelyn served an anticoagulant cocktail, I played a prank, and Rupert got what he deserved.

For the love of a daughter

Catherine Scott Bell

You're going to show me the insides of a sheep?

You're old enough now, Ruby.

Which parts? she asks.

Everything, he replies.

Even the wee bag?

The young girl swings her skinny body up onto the wooden railing. Perched like a sparrow with a ringside seat, she watches her father sharpen and sterilise the blades.

He hardly notices her. His eyes bear down on the tools neatly arranged on the metal tray in front of him. She, on the other hand, observes his every move, knowing not to make a sound, not to distract her father. One false move could draw blood and her father's ire.

She tweaks her nose and inhales the fragrant, grassy, moist smell of the wool shed.

She sighs. This is her happy place, by her father's side, learning from her father.

Her father turns to her, a hacksaw in hand. He is tall and lean, with a permanent limp and a short fuse, the scars of war. His expression is earnest.

But his eyes soften when he gazes down and sees her nosing the air.

It's the smell of lanolin, he explains. It keeps the sheep's wool dry. If you rub your hands along a sheep's back, it will make your hands very soft.

Holding his large, weathered hands out to her, palms wide open, she places her tiny hand in his and whispers the new word in reply:

Lanolin.

Word perfect, he nods.

Her freckled face lights up, and she breaks into a broad grin.

Then her father limps towards a large, white body bag hanging motionless from the wool shed rafters. The girl's eyes follow him.

He carefully removes the shroud. A sheep's carcass is revealed in all its nakedness, pale and pink, dangling by its front legs, stripped bare of wool and skin.

The girl slides down from the railing and inches silently forward, close enough now to breathe in the raw, sweet smell of flesh.

Her father reaches for the leather butcher's pouch attached to his belt and with a flourish, pulls out a razor-sharp knife. The blade momentarily glints in the sunlight streaming down through a crack in the tin roof.

He plunges the knife into the sheep's flesh, drawing it skilfully down the full length of the sheep's belly. A swift action. A cleanly executed manoeuvre.

With the cavity slit open, the contents escape and quickly tumble into his waiting hands.

The girl holds her breath.

One by one the innards appear: rope-like intestines, a large, slippery red mass of liver, and two small kidneys.

Nothing is wasted. Her father flings the intestines out the back window to the waiting dogs. The liver and kidneys are set aside in a clean metal bowl. She has seen her mother fry kidneys, and liver with bacon, for her father's breakfast.

Then the stomach is removed. It resembles a large purse. He examines it and turns to the child.

Reticulum. Rumen. Omasum. Abomasum: the four compartments of the stomach, Ruby. They help to break down and digest all the grass the sheep eats.

Her eyes grow larger.

Do I have four stomachs?

No, humans only have one stomach.

She rolls the strange words around in her mouth, struggling to perfect the mantra.

Lanolin. Reticulum. Rumen. Omasum. Abomasum.

Other organs arrive with a gush and plop in a messy pile on the wool shed floor. Viscous liquid splashes her gumboots, and the strong, fleshy odour hits her nostrils again.

She squeals with delight. Her father doesn't respond. He concentrates on the task in hand.

Leaning in closer still, the girl waits. The prize exhibit is yet to appear.

When her father cradles the bladder in his cupped hands, the girl is unable to contain her excitement. She giggles and giggles. Her little body shakes with glee.

There it is! The wee bag! The wee bag!

The man corrects his daughter.

Bladder, Ruby. It's called the bladder.

The heart is next. He removes it from the carcass with tender hands, making sure it doesn't fall to the floor.

We need to treat the heart with care, Ruby.

She looks earnestly at her father waiting for his explanation.

He doesn't have the words for matters of the heart, for the love he feels in his heart for his daughter. Instead, he explains its purpose.

The heart pumps blood around the body, Ruby, all day, and all night. It's the hardest working muscle in the body.

She speaks confidently. She wants her father to be proud of her.

Lanolin. Reticulum. Rumen. Omasum. Abomasum. Bladder. Heart. I've learnt seven new words today.

His eyes crinkle. A smile flickers across his face as he ruffles her hair. He is proud of his work too.

He cleans and wraps the knives in a piece of thick hessian sacking, and hands the parcel to his daughter.

You're growing up, Ruby.

They leave the woolshed. She carries her trophy in her outstretched hands, looking straight ahead, walking taller.

He carries the weight of the carcass on his shoulders, but the load feels lighter today.

Together, they walk across the paddock towards the farmhouse.

Yellow Daisies
Carolyn Nicholson

The rhythmic sound of the foam roller, gliding paint onto bare walls, helps to settle Daniel's prickly mood and allows the music, playing through his portable speaker, to reach deeper into his soul and smooth his rough edges. Today is no different to any other work day. At least, it shouldn't be, but it feels different and Daniel can't put his finger on why.

It's his third new build job in a row and their predictability is starting to grate. Though empty properties are far easier to paint, they lack personality and warmth. Daniel enjoys spending time in other people's homes, getting to know the occupants' routines, their personalities. He enjoys it even more when there are children in the family. He loves the energy and noise of children, no matter their mood.

His current job is a block of units and Daniel is ready for it to be over. He applies more paint to the roller and moves to the next wall, expertly gliding the roller up and down the wall until the bare plaster is covered in white.

Clear, crisp, fresh white.

Plain, boring, dull white.

'What's with me today?' Daniel asks.

The only reply is the thud, thud, thud of a tail on tiles as Jock, Daniel's twelve-year-old Border Collie, sensing a break coming, stirs.

'Come on, mate. Let's stretch those legs of yours.' Daniel ruffles the fur on Jock's head and the two go outside.

Daniel stretches his back then pours himself a coffee from his red tartan, steel thermos. Battered and chipped, the thermos was a gift from his mother when he started his apprenticeship, sixteen years ago and it still works as well as it did then. Well, almost. Daniel chooses to ignore the fact that his coffee is lukewarm by lunchtime and cold by mid-afternoon. After all, how hot does he really need his coffee to be?

He leans against his pickup truck and sips his now cold coffee. He watches Jock as he sniffs his way round the yard, looking for the perfect spot to relieve himself. The wind blows across a daisy bush and the flowers dance in the sunlight. His thoughts drift to his mother, Maggie, and Daniel reminds himself to visit her on the way home. It's been five days since his last visit and he never goes a week without seeing his mother. His rock. His hero. His only living parent.

A song catches Daniel's attention, he nods his head to the familiar tune of Part Time Believer by Boy and Bear. Today's playlist contains all their albums but it's been some time since he's heard this particular track. The tempo builds as it leads into the chorus and Daniel feels his emotions souring with the music.

The chorus speaks of a boy, sitting on his balcony, waiting for his dad to come home from work so he can show the chords he has learned to play on his guitar. Daniel thinks back to the day he was waiting for his own dad to come home from work; a day he will never forget.

***

'Come on, Danny, you'll be late for school,' Maggie calls out from the kitchen.

'Just two more minutes. I've nearly got it,' fifteen year-old Daniel replies. His face is a picture of focus and attention.

'Will you take him today?' Maggie asks her husband, Rob. 'I need to get to work. You can drop him at the bus stop on the way to the site.'

'Sure,' comes Rob's easy reply. He smiles across his mug at Maggie. His high school sweetheart and the love of his life. 'Anything for you my love.'

Maggie chuckles. 'Thanks.' She kisses Rob, rests her cheek against his for a moment then walks towards the front door. 'Bye, Danny,' Maggie calls out. 'Your dad will drop you at the bus stop.'

'Bye, Mum,' Danny replies.

Maggie turns back and looks at Rob. 'See you tonight.'

Rob finishes his coffee then rinses the mug in the sink, placing it on the rack to dry.

'Come on, mate. I've gotta go.' Rob calls out as he grabs his keys and cooler bag from the bench.

'I'm ready.' Daniel appears at the door with his school bag on his back and his guitar case in his hand.

'Got rehearsals today?' Rob asks as they walk towards the car.

'Nah. I wanna keep working on the song. I've nearly got it.' Daniel places his case and school bag in the back seat.

'Remind me again, which song.' Rob starts the engine and begins to back out of the drive.

'Come on. It's only the greatest song on the radio at the moment, Boulevard of Broken Dreams, by Green Day. Remember? You showed me the chords for the chorus on Sunday.'

'I'm messing with you, mate.' Rob ruffles Daniel's hair. 'How long 'til the school concert?'

Daniel blows out a breath. 'Two weeks,' he replies. 'Which is why I need to practice. The band will kill me if I don't get it right. I'm still stuck on the tremolo.' Daniel chews his bottom lip.

'You'll be right, mate. We can spend some time on it after dinner tonight.'

'Awesome. Thanks, Dad.' Daniel sits up straighter in his seat. 'Could we go through the whole song a few times, check my timing?'

'You bet.' Rob parks his car near the Blairgowrie shops bus stop. There are students from different schools gathered around the shelter.

'There's Ollie.' Daniel waves to his friend.

'Wait a minute, Danny.' Rob pulls the handbrake up and turns to face Daniel. 'I'm proud of how hard you're working, both with your music and your school work. You're a good kid. When you commit to something, you go all in. That will serve you well when you're older.

'What about we drive up to Allans Music on Saturday, have a look at the Gibson you've been wanting?' Rob asks.

'Seriously?' Daniel's teeth shine brightly in the car's interior as his smile stretches across his face.

'Sure. You've proven your commitment and your birthday's in a couple of months.'

'Wow! Thanks, Dad.' Danny throws his arms around Rob's neck and squeezes, not caring who from the bus stop may be watching. 'You're the best.'

Daniel rushes from the car, calling to Ollie as he drags his bag and guitar case from the back seat. 'Ollie! Guess what? Dad's gonna buy me the Gibson.'

Later that day, Daniel is home from school and is in his bedroom, his guitar resting on his lap. His fingertips, not yet fully calloused, are tender and raw but he desperately wants to impress his Dad and have all the chords right before they practice tonight.

Pausing to stretch his back and shake out his hands, Daniel notices the time. It's five-thirty. Dad should be home by now.

'Mum?!' Daniel calls out.

'In here,' Maggie answers.

Maggie is in the kitchen, listening to music as she prepares their dinner. Daniel recognises a Coldplay song. One of his mum's favourites.

'Where's Dad?' Daniel asks.

'He probably got held up on site.' Maggie looks at the time. 'He should be home soon.'

'He said he'd help me with my song for the concert after dinner.'

'Well, it's not dinner time yet.' Maggie says. She glances at the clock again and frowns.

Daniel goes to the lounge room and turns the television on. Losing himself in an episode of Deal or No Deal he doesn't hear the doorbell, or the strange voices at the door. But there was no missing Maggie's wail.

'Nooo!'

'Mum?! What is it?' Daniel runs towards the sound. There are two police officers in the front hall. Maggie is leaning against the wall. Her hands are covering her face. She is making a noise Daniel has never heard before and hopes to never hear again.

'What is it? What happened?' Daniel rushes to Maggie, wrapping his arms around her. His instinct is to protect his mother from whatever is causing her to make such a raw, guttural sound.

'Mum? Please, Mum. What's wrong?' Daniel glares at the police officers.

One of them takes a step forward.

'I'm sorry, son. There was an accident at your dad's worksite. Your dad was badly injured. I'm sorry to tell you, he died on the way to the hospital.'

And just like that, Daniel's world changed forever.

The sound of Jock barking draws Daniel back to the present day. He wipes a stray tear from his cheek. The pain of losing his dad is always there, just under the surface. He has never stopped missing him. Glancing at his watch Daniel notices the date.

June 2.

Now his mood makes sense. It was June 2, 2005 when Daniel lost his hero. His friend. His father. The day Daniel became a man.

Daniel knows what he needs to do; where he needs to be and decides to cut his workday short. He quickly packs up his equipment.

'Come on, mate,' he calls to Jock as he opens the driver's door. Jock leaps from the driveway and across to the passenger seat. The drive home is short and within fifteen minutes he walks through his front door. He goes straight to the spare room. He drags a couple of boxes out of the way and reaches under the bed. His hand searches for the metal handle. Finding it, he wraps his fingers around it and pulls, dragging the case from under the bed.

Daniel flicks the latches and opens the case. Inside is the Gibson guitar Maggie bought him for his sixteenth birthday, two months after his dad died. Daniel hasn't played it in years. He never did perform at the school concert. But he did play Boulevard of Broken Dreams. Once. At his father's funeral. With tears streaming down his cheeks and his eyes on his father's casket Daniel played the song. He didn't miss a chord.

The song, once a source of joy, became an ode to the pain and loss Daniel felt after his father died. A reflection of the depth of his sadness, of his grief, of his loneliness.

Daniel strums the strings, moving his fingers along the frets. He takes a few minutes to re-tune and re-connect with his guitar before putting it back in the case. He stands, the case hits the side of his leg.

'Not this time, Jock. Stay!' Daniel gives Jock a scratch behind the ear before walking back out to his truck, guitar case in hand.

'How is she today?' Daniel asks.

'A little unsettled,' replies the worker.

Daniel enters his mother's room. 'Hi Mum. You look lovely today.' Not wanting to scare Maggie, Daniel doesn't greet her with a kiss, but gently touches her arm. He removes last week's flowers from the vase sitting on the timber television cabinet and replaces them with a fresh bunch of Maggie's favourite flowers, yellow daisies.

Daniel sits in a chair opposite Maggie. She is yet to acknowledge his arrival. Diagnosed with early-onset Alzheimer's at fifty, now fifty-eight, Maggie is mostly lost to the disease.

He places the guitar case on his lap and once again flips the latches. He removes the Gibson and strums the strings a few times, checks the tuning.

'I love you, Mum.' Daniel places his fingers on the frets and begins to play Maggie's favourite song, Yellow by Coldplay.

He watches Maggie closely as he continues playing. Recognition dances across her features. A spark of awareness brings light back into her eyes; her mouth curls into a smile.

'I love you too, Rob,' Maggie replies.

Wandiligong
Zachary Pryor

Leslie stood in the kitchen. Pensive, stiff, watching how the warm afternoon sun danced across the long dining table. The muttering and occasional swearing from Graham outside broke her concentration. He was raking up the leaves that threatened to smother the backyard in a flood of brown. A fruitless endeavour; pyrrhic victory. His war with the shades of autumn.

She carefully unpacked the eggs from the hessian Woolworth's bag, placing them from the carton into the plastic moulds in the fridge door. Spinach followed, then milk, oat milk for Chloe, apples, grapes, bananas, steaks for dinner, eggplant for Chloe. She drummed her fingers on the bench, the marble made a soothing clomp. Heat prickled at her cheeks, and she pursed her lips. Wine, yes, she needed wine. She moved several bottles from the rack to the fridge. More swearing from outside.

She called out to her husband. Beer in hand. They'd be here any minute. Chloe had rung yesterday to say her boyfriend Kenji was stuck in Melbourne, spending Easter with his family. On the phone, Leslie had smiled, the briefest flicker of pleasure pulsed through her, not that she didn't like Kenji, but it was the first time her children would be back under one roof, without the additional extras, the people they'd met along the way, what a treat to have just them for Easter.

She'd really been feeling the distance living out here, they hadn't trekked into Melbourne all year and they weren't together for Christmas. With their new home still in the throes of construction, they'd flown to Sydney to be with Leslie's sister. Chloe stayed in the city, celebrating with Kenji's family. And Perry? Having flunked off the last two semesters of uni to follow some girl overseas, he'd been traipsing around Bali and Vietnam and Cambodia. Graham would purple every time they talked about it. Blotchy red would creep up his face and Leslie would grab a beer or rub his neck and remind him he was only young, and travel wasn't forever, and he'd still have plenty of time to get through medicine.

It was Chloe who arrived first, naturally. She burst through the door, holding her pillow, with her Country Road duffel slung over one shoulder. Bubbly bottle blonde.

'Mum!' she cried as she walked down the steps and into the cavernous living area with high, high ceilings, where Leslie was frantically packing away the shopping bags. She looked up, moving wispy bits of hair from her forehead. 'The place looks great–so much bigger than the photos.'

Chloe dumped her belongings at the foot of the stairs. Her boots made a muted thunk against the polished concrete as she strode across to the kitchen bench to embrace her mother.

'Sorry, I've barely had time to clean up,' Leslie said. Flowers needed to be stemmed and dunked in water, books needed to go back on the shelf, the tea-towel needed to be returned to the oven. 'I thought you were bringing Perry?'

'He got caught up working an early shift, he's coming later. Where do you want these?' she pointed to her belongings. She'd need to move them before Graham came inside.

'I'll show you round. When were you last here?'

'January? We stayed at your rental though.'

'That's right, God time flies–we officially moved in Feb!' Leslie exclaimed. 'The decks now finished, we've done so much landscaping, laundry's done, kitchens finished, bedrooms finished. All the bathrooms are up and running, except ours–faulty plumbing.' She stopped. Her mouth had gone dry.

'Mum.'

'Your father doesn't love the colour of the rooms–says they're too white. Sterile. Said it reminds him of the hospital he interned at. So, that's changing. And my retreat still needs plaster, furniture.'

'Relax. It's perfect.' Chloe took her hand.

'Come, I'll show you where you're sleeping.'

She picked up Chloe's bag, her pillow, and motioned for her to follow her down the hallway to the bedroom. She'd found one of Chloe's old teddy bears, salvaged from the purge they did before they sold their place in Sandringham. Living out here, she did miss the water, the gentle lap of the waves on the shore, the soft sand digging between her toes, their old dog Lotto, bounding ahead, coat of gold gleaming in the sun. Though, the mountain air was cleansing, therapeutic.

'Brownie.' Chloe picked up the bear and stroked its ear. 'It's been a while, old girl.'

Chloe unzipped her boots and unpacked her bag. Leslie twirled the throw over the bed again, fingered off a lick of dust from the bedside lamp. She tucked Chloe's pillow behind the decorative cushions.

'You're still a vegetarian, yes?' She picked at the nail of her index finger.

Chloe swivelled around. 'Dad's not going to give me shit about it, is he?'

'Language.' Leslie inhaled sharply. 'No. No. Just checking, he wanted steaks, I've got you an eggplant.' It was as she said this, she realised she'd withdrawn into the corner, and she was absentmindedly staring out the window to the lawn, where Graham was dumping the last of the crunchy leaves into a polyethylene garden bag. She straightened and told her daughter there were fresh towels in her ensuite. Take your time, unwind, that's why we live out here, the serenity!

'It's great to see you, Mum.' Chloe threw her arms around her, digging her face into the crook of her neck, holding her close. Leslie inhaled her daughter's sweet perfume, squeezed her arm, then made her way into the heart of the house to hand Graham that beer.

Perry arrived shortly after six, bursting through the house and waltzing down the stairs. How long had it been? Seven? No, eight. No! Nine months since they'd seen him. His hair was shaggier, lighter, and three new tattoos snaked up his forearm. The sun had left its celestial fingerprints all over him, as if soaked in golden watercolours.

Leslie showed Perry his sleeping quarters. He said he needed a shower and he spoke with a soft lilt, almost a drawl, each word considered and pregnant on his tongue. Stoned? He wouldn't be so stupid, so careless, he knew better–his father would have a fit. Send him to the corner like he did when he was a child, make him stand in time-out, back to the room, even if he needed to go to the bathroom. Let him stand in his own filth. Leslie shivered and ran her fingers through her hair, handed her son a towel and closed the door behind her.

A chill rushed through the house. Graham rested on the squat, bulbous armchair. Phone in hand, legs propped on the ottoman, halfway through his third tin. Chloe lounged in the opposite armchair, legs slung over the end, absorbed in a book, half a glass of wine finished. A familiar rhythm. Silence. Punctuated only by the soft trill of Brahms flowing from the speakers, hoisted into the ceiling last week.

In the kitchen, Leslie finished a salad. Sliced cucumber, tomato, red onion, mixed olive oil, lemon juice and squeezed Dijon mustard into a jam jar, shaken violently before spilling over the leaves. She rubbed the steaks and eggplant in salt and pepper and laid them onto the grill. The sizzle and rising scent prompted an immediate Pavlovian response. Her hands trembled as she flipped over the meat.

They were here. All of them. Under their roof. Their new Colorbond steel roof.

'There's my boy,' Graham said as Perry returned to the fray, jumping up, knees clicking as he stretched. Her husband's nose wrinkled at the tattoos. He embraced his son and ruffled his hair. Perry recoiled slightly, like a filament flickering in the bulb.

'Mum, you need help with anything?' he asked, helping himself to a beer.

She shooed him away, saying everything was taken care of and dinner was ready, sit up–please, it'll get cold. Leslie danced around–napkins, condiments, topping up wine, opening beer, flicking out Brahms for something jazzy, upbeat.

'Sit down, Mum,' Chloe said, gently scolding. 'You're stressing me out.'

'It's so good to see you both,' Graham said, between mouthfuls, the folds of his neck shaking. 'Even if one of us is still eating rabbit food.' He eyed Chloe, who petulantly returned his gaze, putting down her knife and fork.

'It feels good to finally be settled, it's been a long project.' Leslie smiled. There was still so much to do.

Words slipped past each other. Uninterrupted stories. Perry filling in the blanks from his tour of Vietnam, kayaking in Halong, friends he'd made in Ho Chi Minh, the excursion into Laos. A real adventure, he seemed older, wiser, Leslie wondered if the taste of travel had changed him, if he was ready to settle back into his studies, or if he was itching to take off again–this time further, the destinations wilder, more remote.

'And, Mum–you having time to write?' Perry asked.

Leslie shook her head. 'Only a little–I've been so busy, but I will.' She'd been promising everyone she'd finish her novel soon, soon. Something she'd been telling people since Perry was crawling. She thought ruefully of her retreat, the books still in boxes, the room unplastered, the monitor still in its box from Officeworks.

'I've had a bit of a read–not bad, still needs a lot of work,' Graham said.

Leslie sat up, stunned. 'You have? When?'

'You leave your laptop lying around, thought I'd look at the bloody thing you've been banging on about for the last two decades.'

Deep crimson prickled at her cheeks. No one had seen her work. These were her intimate thoughts, the collection of characters so close to her she knew their secrets, their every thought, their every movement. A family on the precipice of change. It wasn't ready for anyone.

'You could have told me.' She masked her discomfort with a smile.

Graham grabbed her arm, squeezing it, and she tensed. 'Got a long way to go, but you'll get there, baby. You have all the time in the world to write, now we have our little oasis.'

Resentment curled its fingers in her gut. Blood surged and her toes clenched. She wanted to toss the wine in his face. Instead, she addressed the table: 'What does everyone want to do this weekend?'

Leslie woke to overcast clouds, thick in the sky, charcoal on the horizon. She laced her running shoes and hit the path that snaked behind their house. She ran through a reserve, past the pine tree plantations, down to the creek and onto the main road.

In mid-2020, they'd purchased this scrap of land eight minutes outside Bright in an area she'd never heard of. Wandiligong was a sleepy village tucked away in a valley, famed for chestnut festivals and a red Chinese swing bridge erected in 2003 to honour those who worked the land during the gold rush. Seduced by the articles they'd shared with each other back and forth on The Design Files; this cute little ranch, that cute little station, cute little orchards for potential grandchildren to run around in, duck shell blue weatherboards, yearning for adventure, tree change, easing slowly into retirement surrounded by the glory of the Alpine Shire, and of course, exhausted by the dull monotony of lockdown(s).

On this scrap of land, they could escape, reconnect, unwind, and enjoy each other into the twilight of their lives. Jesus, they were barely past sixty! But Graham had worked hard, Leslie had worked hard raising the kids, they'd earned this–they kept telling each other this, their children this, the architect, builder, plumber, sparkies, and other finishing ser-vices, as they began the construction on their dream home that would last several years.

The mountain air was sharp, dewy, of promise and renewal. The peo-ple in the town had been so welcoming, asking after her family, old life in the city, stopping her for chats in the supermarket, wanting them to join in the activities at the Bright Community Centre (birdwatching, scrabble, wool crafts!), excited another couple had migrated to the Shire. This made it easier on the days that she was filled with uncer-tainty.

When Leslie returned home a little after seven, the clouds had turned darker, darker, with them came gusting winds, harassing the trees. She made it inside as the drizzle started.

They were a family of early risers. Chloe was back in her armchair, powering through another book about an Australian family living on a remote island in Scotland who stumbled upon a selkie–Leslie read it earlier in the year and sent a copy. Perry was distracted by his phone, stooped over the bench. Graham was buttering toast. He greeted her with a kiss, asking if she wanted coffee.

'Thought I could take the kids to see Mum,' he said. Both Chloe and Perry looked up. Leslie grabbed a mug, nodding.

Their grandmother lived thirty minutes away in an aged care facility in Myrtleford. Part of the condition of moving out here, to this remote, scenic, peaceful part of Victoria, was that Graham could be close to his beloved mother for the last years of her life. With her mind half lost to dementia, each day was like navigating a maze. She never cared for Leslie when she was lucid, but senility had brought with it cruel insults levelled at her 'quiet, fumble-mouthed, spoiled daughter-in-law'. Gra-ham brushed it off, saying it was all nonsense, but Leslie caught her on numerous times rolling her eyes or sneering or once, pulling the finger.

'Sounds lovely, you don't mind if I skip it?' Leslie said, wiping crumbs off the bench. 'I'll check on her next week.' That should make up for her absence. Graham always expected her to pop in, make sure she was comfortable, and Leslie was running out of ways to say no.

Thunder crackled and the drizzle transformed into a downpour that didn't relent for the rest of the day. The house was steeped in gloom. With her family gone for the afternoon, she went to her retreat at the end of the house. The walls were unfinished, hollow. She had dreams of painting them lilac, fixing a lock to the door, unpacking the books, sitting on cushions and sipping wine, keeping the world and the occupants of their house out, so she could steal small moments to herself. Small moments that would become hours, days, weeks, of silence, just her–with her ideas. Saturnine stillness washed through her as she pictured what she would do to the space.

Would it ever be done? Building this house was supposed to be joyful–a way to bring them closer together, but there had been issues about the layout and landscaping and carpet and kitchen configurations. Graham, as usual, got his way. Then it had been supply-chain issues and rising costs and labour shortages and Graham had to take more locum shifts at the local clinic to get some more cash. Her retreat, it seemed, would remain forgotten forever, the last room on their priority list.

She had a vegetarian shepherd's pie already in the oven when they got home. Warmth from the heater pressed through the living room. The curtainless windows were all inky–the dark turned them into a mirror, reflecting the room. The curtains, another thing they hadn't been able to decide on! Chloe stumbled through the door first, teary and sunken.

'Nanna's got so much worse, she didn't know who I was.' Chloe's lip trembled, wiping rain off her brow. Leslie gave her a hug, offering cups of tea. Visits to Nanna always rankled Graham. He trudged down the steps after Perry. Their shoes squelched on the floor.

'How was she?' Leslie asked. She placed her hands on her husband's shoulders.

'Same,' he replied, shrugging her off. The bulbs flickered as he switched on the lights to the living area. 'What the?' He jimmied the switch. On. Off. On. Off. Darkness.

'We've been having issues with some of the wiring,' Leslie announced, gripping the bench.

'Can you call someone?' Perry asked.

'No—no,' Graham replied, defiant. 'Something isn't right, I need the contractor back. Wait till John hears about this. Fuck.' He stomped his foot.

Everyone flinched.

'We've still got the hallway, kitchen and dining light—we'll be fine.' Leslie quivered.

'Lucky you guys have that white privilege thing of too much space and open plan living,' Chloe winked, as she walked away. 'I'm going to my room, haven't spoken to Ken all day.' And she was gone.

Graham paced, staring at the ceiling and back to Leslie. Another thing. Another cost. Another small niggle. Another little chink to their perfect little nest.

'Honey...' she said in a soothing tone. Tension coiled in her belly.

'Excuse me, Leslie.' He collapsed into his big chair and closed his eyes. The breathing was deep, laboured. Then, with his eyes closed, he said: 'Perry, at some point we're going to need to talk about your education.'

Perry rolled his eyes. She caught him, as if to say—not now, it'll be alright, but we need to have the talk.

'Yes, Dad.' Perry said. 'Can we do it later? I'm going to take a shower. I've got that old people's home stench.'

Graham leaped to his feet. 'What did you say, boy?' The vein above his temple throbbed.

'Nothing.' Perry retreated.

Graham's meaty hands grabbed his forearm, twisting and pulling it towards him. 'Show some respect.' His teeth bared.

He released him. Perry stood taller, defiant, staring him down, lip curling. Living with Graham was sometimes like living inside a headache. He'd gotten better, yes—over time he'd practiced patience and meditation, but every now and then he'd snap. Perry took a step forward when the buzzer from the oven trilled.

♥ ♥ ♥

Saturday brought with it clear skies and sunlight. Frost that spilled into limned radiance. After her run, she took Perry on a walk up a hidden path through the plantation. There was a gentle heat giving the autumnal scene a sort of distance, the sense that it had been frozen, that time was moored.

As she walked, she pondered this scene–that autumn offered a feeling of hope, rather than a conclusion. They made their way up through the pine trees and reached a lookout.

'Dad wants me back at school, but I'm unsure,' Perry said. He'd spent most of the walk talking about his options–finish med, maybe switch into biomedical science, or maybe pharmacology–but she could tell, by how he trailed off, how his voice lacked inflection, that his heart wasn't in it.

'You know I just want you to be happy, but you're only twenty–take the time to figure it all out.'

'Does he know that?'

'Let me deal with your father.'

'Following him into general practice is his dream.'

'And what's yours?'

Perry paused. He surveyed the landscape. She stood next to him, struck by the softness of the Alpine Shire and the changing quality of light, the patterns of leaves, vibrant and ochre against the sky.

'I'm going to do what I want. I want to work as a tour guide overseas. Maybe Sail Croatia?' He scratched his arm, his forehead squinted. 'I just don't want to let you down, Mum.'

Her poor child. Caught between disappointment and joy. Wanting so little but the freedom to explore the limitations of his world, to go as far as he could, stretch the boundaries, and find out who he was supposed to become. She guessed. She didn't know. She didn't really know who she wanted to become, but the peacefulness of Wandiligong and this risk they'd taken moving out here at least offered her a reprieve.

They reached home. Chloe looked up from her armchair when they walked in, book clutched to her chest. She dropped it onto the coffee table, declaring it the best thing she'd read all year.

'I'm so pleased,' Leslie beamed.

'And that twist!' Chloe stood up.

Leslie scanned the room, peering out the long oblong kitchen windows to the garden. 'Where's your father?'

'On the phone to John.' Chloe replied vaguely. 'Ken says hi.'

Leslie tsked, rubbing the thin white scar running across the top of her left hand, beneath the groove of her knuckles. He couldn't even wait until the end of the weekend. 'Do you know how long they've been talking?'

'Not long. He seemed angry.'

Her face contorted with worry. 'It'll be fine, it'll all be fine.'

Perry pipped in. 'Do you know what we're doing for lunch?'

'We thought we could take you down to the Wandi.' It was a small pub at the end of their street, the last stop on Morses Creek Road. Best in the area, that's what all the locals said. Graham loved to head down there on a Friday afternoon for pints, check out the scene, he'd say, meet new mates, catch some live music, usually cover bands, three guitars and a whole lot of Fleetwood Mac. Leslie had joined him a few times. She thought the festoon lights slung up through the oak trees offered a touch of whimsy.

Graham entered the room. He looked like he was going to hurl his phone at someone. A grenade about to explode. Before he could say anything, Leslie approached him, reminding him of the plan to head down to the pub. A small smile crept up his face.

'Yes, I'll call them. Bloody Easter tourists–hopefully they'll have a spot for us locals,' he said. He found their number and punched it into his phone. He turned his back to them as he answered. 'You're joking!' he exclaimed after several minutes. 'God damnit.'

'What is it, Dad?' Perry asked, cautious.

'Closed! Owners have gone into Melbourne for the weekend. Are you bloody kidding me?' He slammed his phone on the bench. His expression hardening. Leslie glanced at her children, thinking quickly.

'There's the brewery in Bright,' she said, optimistic, hoping Graham would take the offer. 'Lets all get ready, we'll go there.'

'Sure, whatever.' Graham sulked, moving outside to something in the yard that caught his attention.

Leslie went to change. Last week, she'd put up some of their framed photos. On the wall across from her side of the bed she'd hung a blown-up canvas photograph from their wedding day, twenty-five years ago. Graham still had a full head of hair, his face slimmer, kinder, he hadn't grown into his paunch yet. She was whispering into his ear–what did she say? She couldn't remember now, but she loved how happy they looked, salubrious smiles, shared intimacy, shared secrets, how they would build this life together, one she didn't know she wanted, but one she didn't know how to live without, one she didn't know how she could afford to live without.

She shrugged off her sweater, her Lululemon leggings and fetched a loose cotton dress from the wardrobe. She'd buttoned it up when a thud and a loud bellow came from outside. And another scream. Her husband!

She rushed out to the deck, where Graham lay flat on his back cursing. Chloe and Perry followed her. She placed her hands around Graham's head.

'Honey, what happened?' She motioned to Perry to help, and the two of them slowly sat him up. He twinged and wriggled and spasmed, rubbing his lower back and breathing, breathing. They moved him inside and onto the couch, where they lay him down. Chloe handed him a glass of water.

'Slipped, leaves on the deck,' he said through gritted teeth. His chest heaved with exertion.

'Stay here, don't move.' Leslie made herself useful. She wrapped frozen peas in a tea towel and handed them to him. He pressed them to his back, wiping away stinging tears.

'Let me see,' he wheezed, slowly getting to his feet before he cried out in pain and collapsed back onto the couch. 'Fuck me.'

'Dad, is there anything we can do?' Chloe asked, fretful, peering over her mother's shoulder.

'You guys go, go–have lunch, go for a wine tasting at Billy Button's, don't ruin your day on account of me. I'll be fine.'

'Are you sure?' Perry said, supressing a smile.

Leslie bent down to kiss Graham's cheek before grabbing the car keys and ushering her children out the door.

Later that evening, after games of Monopoly Deal were won and lost, dinner was eaten and dishes tidied away, she tucked Graham into bed. He was still twitching, moving stiffly. He'd knocked back a handful of ibuprofens with some whisky to numb the pain and passed out within minutes. Now he rested on his back, propped up by several pillows, snores rumbling.

Leslie lay next to him, engrossed in a book about a cannibalistic food critic living in Los Angeles. Despite (or because of) Graham's injury, she had to admit, they'd had a wonderfully pleasant day. A long lunch with the kids at the local brewery on the banks of Ovens River, then they stepped into a cellar door and sampled obscure white wine varietals. She'd asked Chloe questions about her grad position at ANZ, she asked more questions about Kenji, and whether they were going to move in together. Walking through the town she pointed out the bookstore and artisanal homeware shop she loved, she stopped by a community notice board and saw a flyer advertising a local writer's group, she ripped off one of the tags with the number for the organiser. Yes, it was about time she took this little hobby seriously. The few hours spent alone with her children made the pull and tug of them leaving tomorrow to head back to their busy lives in Melbourne all that more unbearable.

She put down her book and dashed to the bathroom to brush her teeth. A blue glow emitted from the television in the living room and hushed voices caused her to stop in the hallway. She could just make out what her children were muttering.

'I want more days like this with her,' said Chloe.

'Wish it could just be the three of us,' Perry whispered.

'Yeah.'

'She seems like she's doing better, though. We had a big walk today—you can tell she really loves it here.'

'But she's so alone!'

'She's always making friends—did you see her chatting to that lady at the bar? Been here for a few months and already knows everyone.'

'Perry.' Chloe said with the unmistakable sternness of an eldest chiding their younger sibling. 'But did you see her arms?'

A pause. Then Perry said mournfully, 'I thought he stopped?'

'So did I.'

'He's such an arsehole.'

Her heart caught in her throat. Hand pressed to her mouth. Ribs constricted. Shame pulsed through her body. She slipped into the bathroom. Secrets bubbling inside her, bursting, words spoken out loud by her children—the knowing, the fear.

Hot tears dampened her face. She pressed her palms to her cheeks to catch them. Her breathing was shaky, interrupted.

Leslie grabbed a tub of arnica from the vanity and rubbed it in a tidy circular motion over the rainbow of bruises colouring her upper arms. A whiff of the pine-sage ointment filled her nostrils. Her eyes closed and she searched for the past. She recalled the contusions and teeth marks on her neck that she'd once covered with an orange silk scarf. Her fingers slammed in the bedroom door. That sickening crunch. The screams. The pleading. Hair pulling. The hum from her bones with each smack. The metallic tang of blood bursting in her mouth. The years and years and years and years.

Of course, not her husband—her outwardly kind, patient husband. That upstanding pillar of society who'd devoted his life to medicine, to families that made up his Beaumaris clinic, who talked through their concerns about health and made referrals. No. No one would have ever believed her.

Leslie shook her head, blinked through the memories, and placed the arnica back into the cupboard. She grabbed her toothbrush and scrubbed. She would contact their contractor, she would finish her retreat, she would unbox her monitor, she would hide her laptop, she would attend that writer's group at the Bright community centre, she would, she would, she would.

She waited, listening to the footsteps, mugs chinking in the sink, dishwasher whirring, the easy sounds of goodnight, goodnight. Graham's porcine snoring in their bed down the hall. Cold seeping through the crack in the door. The lights in the house flicking off. And the rain starting again, a light patter on the roof. Even. Slow. The roar of it becoming heavier in the distance. She returned to her room.

The Happy Medium
Jane Leonard

They sit facing each other. A train goes by. The younger one leans forward looking around the lounge room. *She's doing well for herself*, she mutters suspiciously inside her head, glancing back at the other, older one. Then nervously down at her cup, *what if I change my life because of a cup of tea?*

The older other one smiling back, not saying, but still they both hear: *Well then, it's meant to be.*

The other older one

No matter what put on the pot I heard Mum say, just after I was conceived. God knows how I knew, when I was no more than a few sticky cells, that as the kettle whistled for my beginning, she, dressed in a chenille robe, wrote *Let this one have a nice life* in biro on the tag of an Earl Grey teabag. Then she and the kettle baptized the sacred little thing in boiling water, and ceremoniously dunked and squeezed it, and she blessed herself, *Bless me*, as she flung it past the kitchen curtains, into the universe, above the geraniums, tag whizzing behind like the tail of a comet, into the leaves of the lemon tree, where I saw (I don't know how) it dangle next to a ripe lemon, and felt Mum sit and clasp the cup with both hands and sigh and smile. I increased and came and somehow always knew from then on, everything that was going to happen to everyone.

As a babe I brimmed with pop-the-kettle-on resilience, and have-another-cup-dear optimism, which made Mum smile more, because she knew that what she wished for was going to come true. She taught me everything she knew, *Start the day with an Earl Grey, end it with a chardonnay*, and how to write my dreams upon my teabags and fling them, wing them, she holding my shoulder pointing at the lemon tree out the back, such a vision splendid, laden with her fears and hopes, tags flapping gently like Chrissy decorations.

As I grew, I flung myself at my own first tiny china tea set, and with imaginary brews, I knew, I knew, what was really true. I only had to fill the pot to know what's what, to sip the cup to know what's up. It didn't surprise Mum when a lady came to the door one day, selling encyclopedias. She leaned around and pointed: *That girl knows!* Mum, nodding, replying *come in for a cuppa*, the leaves of which were read, with stuff said, about what I was going to be when I grew up. And so, I began to read, not books but cups. I didn't understand at first, I just noticed that, when I made the tea, everything became clear and strong, nothing wrong, Mum asking me stuff, tender, then *Had enough?*

With each brew I grew and eventually I went. Mum and me still shared tea, on my own porch now, watching proud, as the paperboy on his pushie scored a bullseye, making my sign *The Happy Medium (Tea Leaf Readings)* swing cheery in the sun, and it came to me that boy is going to do fine which he did. And so did I, kettle singing, reading, telling, them all coming, going, looking round my lounge room.

She's doing well for herself, they'd mutter suspiciously inside their heads, glancing back at me, then nervously down at their tea, *what if I change my life because of a cup of tea?* Me smiling back, not saying, but still they hear: *Well then, it's meant to be.*

Then that one day, the day of the saddest cup of tea in my life, thousands of pots and a cozy or two down the way, after a sip, I see me, my Mum, my Mum and me. My Mum with a big grin, even though she's sick and thin, Good Old Mum, there behind my eyes. At her insistence, I lift up the crocheted cozy and rub the teapot like a genie's lantern, and out she comes, young Mum, well Mum, smelling of Earl Grey, softened by boiling kettle mist. And I know, I know, even though I don't want to with all my might, that Mum is gone, for good, for good alright, and after getting out the special china and my favorite pot, I put four full kettles on the stove and weep when they sing, starting with a sigh, first one, then back-left, and front-right, all raising their voices till my whistle begins to go, and I join them in their desperate high-pitched chorus, until my heart boils, and then calms, the heat turned off, the kettles and me quietening gently to silence, my tears dripping into the brew, thanking Mum with all my heart for this life so nice I had, (*Let this one have a nice life*) that she gave me, written on a tag.

I write in smudged Texta back, *Let that one have a nice death* and fling it farther than ever before, over the railway lines, into the paddock of wildflowers and weeds where we used to sometimes meet with a thermos full of lovely tea–*Made with Vitamin L* Mum used to say, *L for Love, its how I always make my tea*. Back inside I see her face, in the bottom of my cup, she's looking up, at me, *Darling, no matter what put on the pot, and have a cuppa tea*.

The younger one

She gave me good tea but not so good news. I don't know why I went. A year before, I'd stood on the nature strip over the road around the corner from Mum's, looking at the beautifully painted teapot sign. *The Happy Medium–Tea Leaf Readings*, with *No Matter What, Put on the Pot* in smaller letters underneath. I stood behind a car, self-conscious, trying to check it out, but not be seen. She was sitting on the front porch having tea with a much older woman. A paper boy went past. He flung a newspaper from his basket over the low fence. It hit the sign dead on, and rattled the chains it hung from. She stood up, raising her cuppa towards the boy. I was surprised at how frumpy she looked in her old-fashioned apron. A bit like my Mum, but perhaps not quite as old. I listened to her yell *Bullseye, Steven! Did I ever tell you you'll do well?* There was no reply from the paperboy already disappearing around the corner. He didn't seem to hear or care. But he remembers her words years after when he has his feet up on a big desk in a tall building and someone good-looking brings him coffee. (Of course, I only know this much later when he comes to me, in an expensive suit, greedy for more predicted success).

Actually, maybe I do know why I went to see her. I wanted her to tell me what I wanted to happen would, or if not, then things better. I wanted confirmation that what wasn't okay, somehow would be. That things would turn out alright. But she didn't say much of anything along those lines. She mentioned this and that, but then dismissed it all with two sniffs and a sip of tea. And then she looked at me strangely, and as I thought of all the stuff I'd been through lately, dealing with Mum's news, the weirdest thing happened: she told me the story of her and her own Mum, her life, her Mum's death. But here's the thing–she told me all in the flicker of an eye, without a single word–I can't explain it.

Afterwards, she laughed, as if she were surprised, and told me that in time, I'd know what I had to do. And in the meantime, she went on telling me, that until I'm ready for all that (*it's quite hard at first*, she winked) that I should write a book, or was it story, or perhaps she said would? Anyway, back then, none of it seemed to have anything to do with anything, and I took no notice. Or so I thought, as I berated myself for wasting my time and money, even though she was sweet.

After, I went round to Mum's. She was sitting at the table and looked sad as she slowly rifled through a box of old photos and knick-knacks. She pulled out a school portrait of me as a girl with plaits. Then an older black and white snap of herself also in plaits. There was no photo of her Mum in plaits, but there was an actual plait, just one, severed, wrapped in old brown paper, tucked into an envelope full of my own hair, exactly the same colour as my grandmothers. It was one of the few things brought from her childhood in Egypt. Sometimes I have the strange sense that despite our different lives, we're the same person in different times. Like singing in rounds, the same lyrics and tune, but starting at different moments, our voices overlapping each other's.

I shared this idea with Mum to ward off one of the heavy, awkward silences that came up a lot then. I had never expected to be lost for words when time was short. And she actually laughed–*I like that idea!* Keen to keep her smiling, I told her I'd just been to visit to The Happy Medium, and when she heard the name, she said: *good name for a book.* And so, I went on to tell her about me supposedly writing a book and we joked about how it would start.

I suggested: *They sit facing each other.*

Mum said: *A train goes by.*

I said: *The younger one leans forward looking around the lounge room.*

Mum said: *She's doing well for herself, she mutters suspiciously inside her head, glancing back at the other, older one.*

I said: *Then nervously down at her cup, what if I change my life because of a cup of tea?*

Mum said: *The older other one smiling back, not saying, but still they both hear: Well then, it's meant to be.*

We laughed for ages and even wrote it down on a serviette. But when the giggles subsided, Mum said quietly, *You should do it.*

What? I'm not a writer!? I replied, *it's just oogie-boogie bullshit, Mum.*

Well, why did you go then, she asked, *what if it isn't?*

I stayed silent. At that point I didn't really understand why I went after all. It's not like I was even into that kind of stuff.

But then Mum started talking about how when you want to decide something, you flip a coin. *Heads for Plan A, Tails for Plan B, but then sometimes, even when you get Heads, it's as clear as day: Fuck it, I'm doing Plan B.*

Sometimes, it doesn't matter if it's bull shit or not, she said gently, you just need to hear stuff, regardless of how or where, or even what you do with it. It might just be what you need to hear to do, or not do whatever it is you need, or want to.

I got up to put the kettle on, and even though we pretended it didn't have a place in our lives, the heaviness around her situation came back. Mum needed a lie down, and when I put her cup of tea down quietly beside her bed before I left, she was already asleep. I did end up writing a story, about the women in my family. It got published and people liked it, but Mum never got to read it.

I don't know why, but I took that lady a copy, she who read my tea leaves that time. Perhaps I thought I would feel out the answer to the question that had been bugging me ever since I saw her first–would I have done it anyway? To this day I can never be sure. Maybe Mum was right. Anyway, she was grateful and excited and said *See?* Out on the porch showing me out, she pointed at the teapot sign still swinging cheerily on its chains.

Don't forget, she winked *You'll be good, I can feel it in my bones.* I laughed awkwardly, and shrugged, pretending I had no idea what she was on about. I still wasn't ready back then.

But in the end, even though it took me a while, and plenty of detours here and there, that's what I do now. People often ask me how it came about, and I tell them. They are always suspicious, politely or aggressively, trying to work out if I'm a weirdo, a scammer, a charlatan, or figure out what is true about it all and what is not. But either way, I'm doing alright. People want to come. No one has complained yet. Still, some of my friends endlessly attempt to untangle whether she caused it all, or I, or if it would've just happened regardless. Who knows? I think of Mum and her coin flipping tale. It doesn't matter anyway.

But what if, asks a friend, *you ended up changing the entire course of your whole life just because of a cup of tea?*

I lean back, take a lovely sip of my Earl Grey, and reply *Perhaps then, it was just meant to be.*

Nothing to See Here
Carolynne Hamilton

'Michael, I want to discuss something with you.'

Sarah called this out from her place on the sofa. She had the last minutes of the 'Footy Show' playing on television, its flickering light played on her honey blonde bob. A multi-tasker, she also had her laptop open on her knees and company papers spread about her.

Michael looked up from his canvas, paintbrush poised. He had his easel set up on their impressive balcony and was working in a pool of light cast by an oversize outdoor globe.

'Sure. Shall I stop this? Pour us some more wine?'

He nodded at the open bottle of Chardonnay on the dining table. They had both remarked on its spicy palate. Lighted candles were beside it, plus some soft cheeses coming to room temperature on the marble platter they'd found in Sydney.

'No. No. You can paint and listen, can't you? Besides, I really hate that you always stop what you're doing when I talk to you.'

Michael frowned. Being fully present was a long-held practice, but he let her complaint slide and loaded his brush with Thalo blue. He was practising a technique to create rolling waves.

Sarah snapped her laptop shut.

'I don't think you and I want the same things Michael.'

He tried a delicate swoosh of the brush.

'How so honey?'

'Well, I'm thinking you believe what we have is leading us to something permanent.'

Michael paused the inspection of his brush stroke and looked again at Sarah.

'What do you mean?'

'Well, you act like this arrangement is leading to us retiring and growing old together.'

Michael put the paint brush down. Sarah continued.

'I'm not planning on staying with you Michael. I've considered all my options and I've decided to leave you.'

She wasn't looking at him. She was shuffling papers.

They had not long finished dinner, a meal they had made together, as always. He'd put fresh Atlantic salmon on the Weber™ on the balcony, slipping a titbit to Horatio his beloved Burmese cat. Then he'd worked comfortably hip to hip with her in the kitchen chopping tomatoes and onions for salsa. She had rough cut greens for a salad. They had sipped Hendrick's Gin with tonic and discussed their day. Nothing had been amiss, aside from his moral quandary about whether he should eat any of the cream camembert she'd pilfered from her company kitchen. Over their meal, she'd described a disastrous client meeting and what she'd eaten for lunch at the Springvale Botanical Cemetery. She had not been to a funeral; she just liked how inexpensive the food was.

He loved these quiet evenings in and their meandering conversations about world events, theatre, music and travel spots. He often marvelled at the differing views they had of the world. His was an optimistic outlook; a little fuzzy around the edges whenever Sarah threw her cynical and provocative questions at him. She firmly believed in the importance of money, knowing the right people and the appeal of movement.

Nothing at dinner had prepared Michael for what she had just said. He moved inside to join her on the sofa, but her mess of paperwork forced him to sit on the coffee table in front of her.

'I don't understand Sarah. What do you mean you've decided to leave? Darling. Are you upset about the weekend?'

Their Gold Coast weekend away for her brother's wedding had ended badly. A lavish beachfront affair at a popular resort, it had been an awkward event. He knew no one aside from the bride and groom, and Sarah had disappeared for hours after volunteering to drive older family members home. He spent his time making small talk about property values, financial markets and the Bali nine until he was ready to stab someone with a fork. He had calmed himself by watching the waves roll in and out, observing the colour changes.

Sarah was unaccountably rude when she finally returned. She had wandered among old friends catching up on old times, ignoring his attempts to be introduced. He had tried a few times to get her on the dance floor until finally she'd snapped,

'I've no intention of dancing with you.'

He had danced with her chiffon clad mother whose terrible habit of back leading ruined any chance he had of looking accomplished and desirable on the dance floor.

Later that night, his anger and her aloofness had them sleeping back-to-back.

'No Michael. I'm not upset about the weekend, but I did think about us. I realised this is just holding me back.'

She spread her manicured hands wide to indicate the open plan apartment and themselves. She finally looked at him, her blue eyes hard and features sharp.

'You're too lost in the romance of us as soul mates to ever get beyond this. You're too easily pleased to chase anything else worth having. You just see us as destined to grow old and end our days in a rundown beach house, with paint stains on the rugs and your stupid three-legged cat.'

Michael was listening without comprehending and watching her mouth move. It seemed to have slipped sideways. Words, brown and ugly, spilled out of it, hovered in the air around her, then flitted to the balcony to explode on the giant globe.

'I'm leaving. In a month. It will take me that long to find somewhere else to live. I'll move into the spare room. We like each other, so I don't foresee any issues. When I move out, I'll take furnishings I paid for and that painting we got in London. I'm prepared to be reasonable.'

On saying this, Sarah stood, gathered the paperwork into a file and slid it into her leather tote. She added her laptop then squeezed past him, heading to the dining table. She poured a glass of wine and prodded the cheeses with her finger. Stunned, Michael watched her slice a piece of cheese, place it on a fig and olive cracker and nibble.

'Perfect. You really should try some of this.'

'We changed our wills,' he said quietly as he moved to join her. 'We sat at this table only two months ago and we changed our wills. What was that about if everything we've talked about for our future isn't real?'

Sarah shrugged. 'Paperwork. Means nothing.'

Michael pulled out a dining chair and sat heavily, looking at her in open confusion. Until he'd met Sarah, he'd never thought much about what his future might look like. He was a go with the flow kind of guy. She was the planner. She sat too and leaned across the table to pinch out the candles with her fingertips.

'I don't understand Sarah. You say all the time how much you love me - us. And you hate being alone. I leave you for more than ten minutes, you're on the phone to me and if you can't get me then someone else.'

Watching him impassively, she pulled the cheese platter closer and sliced more cheese. She sipped her chardonnay. He searched her shadowed face, reflected on her detachment and business demeanour. Were her eyes a different colour? Was someone else behind them?

Sarah poured him a glass of wine and topped up her own.

'You should have a drink,' she said.

'I don't want to drink; I want to understand.'

'I'm leaving you. I'm moving out in a month. What's not to understand?'

'But why?'

'I don't want to talk about it. I've got a presentation tomorrow and can't screw it up. I'm going to bed.'

Sarah left him at the table. He stared into his glass of wine; thoughts jumbled. After what felt like the longest time, he stirred himself, wincing as he turned on the lights and set to cleaning everything up. He moved like an automaton. His head was in a fog. He tried and failed to reconcile this Sarah with the woman he'd been loving and living with for the last three years. His adored Sarah was funny, attentive and tender. They had shared their childhood stories and laughed together. They had shared their worst histories and accepted each other. It was she who'd declared them 'simpatico' in what became their favourite Italian restaurant after only two weeks of knowing each other. She'd moved in ten weeks after that; bringing only business suits, designer jeans, 'on trend' T-shirts, and a luminous glass vase that she gifted him as a token of her affection. He'd been hard pressed to keep up with her energetic weekend jaunts, business events and general need to be 'doing something'. He'd slowly won her over to the idea of saving one weekend a month for more reflective activity and introduced her to art exhibitions and opera. They'd fallen into a comfortable if hectic rhythm. He'd slowly withdrawn from his wider circles into their own cosy one.

'What is happening?' he wondered aloud as he wiped bench tops.

Michael turned off the balcony light, the television and sat on the sofa. Horatio clumsily jumped up beside him for some distracted pats. Michael had so many questions, but his anguish made his tongue thick and heart heavy. And she felt like a stranger. Had he ever had a glimpse of this Sarah? He cast his mind back to the early, heady days of their relationship and recalled a peculiar evening when she'd invited him to meet the psychologist he didn't know she'd been seeing. They had driven into a leafy, affluent suburb after dinner, parked in front of a house that real estate agents would promote for its period charm, walked a pathway through extensive lawn to knock on an unremarkable front door. The ageing woman who opened it and ushered them inside was obviously surprised to see them. She had the kind of big eyed, big-cheeked features that disposes people to trust and calmness. There was nothing offensive about her. But she did seem unusually unkempt. Her dirty blonde hair was wiry, big and messy. Her textured winter caftan billowed about her when she walked and sat. She received them in a cosy lounge room with the cliché wall-to-ceiling bookshelves, heavy furniture in muted beige and chocolate browns. There were numerous pot plants showing she embraced the notion that greenery interacts with body, mind and spirit. Her name was Galena, so possibly she'd been fated to live the role of healer.

Michael mostly remembered Sarah showing him off like a trophy, her exuberance and Galena's concern.

'I'm surprised Sarah that you are in a relationship so quickly after your last one ended the way it did. We agreed you'd try living single for two years, yet here you are. With Michael.'

'Yes, I know I agreed to that, but I like talking things over with him. I appreciate his perspective on people, the world. He has a special kind of wisdom and keeps me on an even keel.'

'Are you listening to yourself? If you repeat the choices of the past nothing will change.'

With that last comment, Galena had looked Michael in the eye with what might have been pity. The two women conversed for another half an hour and he got to share some details about himself. As they were leaving Galena had hugged him.

'At least you're a strong person and have a good sense of self,' she said.

Sarah had said her goodbyes with something like triumph on her face. Now, tonight, she was saying goodbye to him.

Michael gently pushed Horatio to the side. He couldn't sit still. He needed to busy himself. He should iron a shirt for work. And some pants. He could hear Sarah in their bedroom opening drawers, wardrobe doors, going to and fro. Suddenly, the apartment didn't feel so spacious. The rage building up inside him felt like it would fill it, the building, the sky. His body, taut and tight was crawling with energy.

Coming from their bedroom, Sarah leaned against the door frame.

'Look at you. So quiet on the sofa,' she said. Then suddenly screamed at him, spittle spraying.

'Why the fuck aren't you smashing plates? You should be smashing plates. I need someone who smashes plates!'

She slapped her hand against the wall again and again and again.

You are so bloody hard to provoke! I've been trying for months, but you're always so bloody calm,' she cried.

'Why on earth do you want to provoke me?'

'Because you make life so fucking easy.'

Later, Michael lay awake and alone in bed. Sarah had moved to the spare room. It was the Byzantium hour when the streets are still, and spirits are restless. He heard Sarah open the bedroom door. Irrationally, he was afraid of and for her. The darkness and her quiet intensity pressed down on him.

'Michael? I know you're still awake. I'm going to take a sleeping tablet. Do you want one?'

She hovered at the door.

'I know this is hard for you, but I'm still your friend. In fact, I want us to stay friends. Michael? You're not going to do anything silly to your-self are you?'

'Please. Just go away.'

He lay awake for hours until he heard the front door open and close, then he rose, fed Horatio, showered and dressed. Automaton once more, he took the tram into the city. He picked up a coffee from his favourite café and arrived in time for his first meeting. No one noticed anything amiss, though the pen shook in his hand as he took notes. Sweat trickled down his back. He felt shaky and nauseous.

'Hold yourself together,' he thought to himself.

During his second meeting, his phone vibrated. It was Sarah. *I didn't tell you everything last night.*

Shaken, he looked quickly at everyone around him. Colleagues all, but not one of them a friend and confidante. *I've been seeing someone for three months.*

Gripping the phone, he excused himself and made his way to the men's room, barely making it to throw up into a toilet. *I'm going to move in with him.*

He splashed water onto his face and ran wet fingers through his hair. How could this be happening, he wondered? We're almost always together. Does she even care how cruelly she's behaving? *I do these things. I don't know why.*

He stabbed out his answer, *What do you want?* and waited for her reply.

Desperate for a cigarette, Michael found himself alone in the elevator, neon bright and sleek with mirrored walls. He was reflected over and over, receding into a tunnel of anguish. He pressed his face into his hands. His shoulders were high and hunched, and his skin hinted faintly pink through his white cotton business shirt.

The elevator stopped, three men entered and looked at him. His dark silence filled the space and curled around them. They turned away to face the elevator door with barely a break in their conversation and one quickly punched the silver floor selection buttons.

Michael's entire body was so tight it felt like it was trying to fold in on itself. His phone vibrated and he jerked upright. A sob tore at his throat as he read Sarah's answer. *The Murano glass vase.*

My heart was won with poetry
Catherine O'Neill

My heart was won with poetry by a gentleman.

It started with words borrowed from the romantics, Shelley and Keats, the old favourites, but they quickly became personal. He wrote rhyming couplets and small stanzas, bright and shiny bubbles that perfectly encapsulated our moments together. His limericks made me laugh, and his sonnets swelled my heart until it burst with love. Our life together, secretly recorded in verse, was a meeting of minds that brimmed with wit and affection, and in the dark of night, desire.

After our first week together, he sent me a postcard from the airport before he left, which arrived in the mail before he landed in London. The handwritten note vowed a swift return, and a week later, he arrived with a gift–a poetry collection called Poems of Love. I held it with reverence, as if it were a sacred text that contained centuries of wisdom; a map for our unconventional journey.

The poems in the sections called Love's Beginnings and Love Fulfilled were read so often, we knew them by heart. The first words he sent to my inbox became like close friends and more were added in the months that followed, as we took turns to read Donne and Tennyson by the fire. The great poets were intoxicating but the cheeky humour of Roger McGough from Summer with Monika was my favourite. My cheeks blazed when I imagined ten milk bottles queued at our door, ignored and in various stages of fermentation, because we, like McGough and Monika, wouldn't leave our bed in the days after we wed.

The poems towards the back of the collection titled In Warning of Love, and Love Lost and Love Remembered held little interest for me then. They had no resonance. I always knew that love would be lost. He would go first. That was the deal I made when I began a life with a man old enough to be my father, but it didn't worry me at the time. Having a mother die in my youth had prepared me, or so I thought. I was ready, armed with experience, able to survive a sudden death and the unending absence where memories were the only comfort.

What I didn't expect was the slow decline, the long fade into someone I no longer recognised. How could I have prepared? I could not have imagined what lay ahead.

We wake as usual, and our silence speaks volumes. Whether it's his habit borne from multiple late night trips to use the loo, or whether it's because we no longer have anything to say, I don't know. He turns the ensuite light on which blinds me, and every morning I regret the choice of a glass door. It was supposed to act like a window, but the light is perfectly angled to shine in my eyes. It is the first irritation of the day. I roll over, to maximise the peace of the bed to myself, even if only for a few minutes.

On the second alarm, I get up, head heavy, eyes caked with sleep. Mascara stains my fingertips, and I am annoyed that I didn't remove it the night before for fear of waking him–my morning's second irritant. I should have gone to bed earlier. I say this every day, and every day, I am an hour short. I'm trying to convince my body it doesn't need that eighth hour, but every five or six days, my body wins and I crash. Only when my eyes cannot stay open for a second longer, when I can do nothing else, will I go to our shared bed.

Lunches are made, breakfast cleared and I get ready for my walk, to escape as much as for the exercise. A pod cast will distract me, inspire more creativity, or produce a sense of calm. Either way, the walk is essential.

He is waiting for the moment I return.

'I'm just about to make some coffee. Would you like some?'

'Thank you, but I'll have a shower first.' Another ten minutes of time on my own. It's what I need to face the day.

'I'll wait.'

The coffee is good, strong, with a thick layer of powdered chocolate on the top. The barista course I arranged for the girls to give him for Father's Day years ago was a stroke of genius. It's the old-age equivalent of giving your spouse a massage course when you're engaged. An ongoing gift to the giver. The process of making coffee, grinding the beans, tamping the coffee into the grip, heating the cups, frothing the milk, cleaning the steam spout and washing the tray, takes up at least half an hour of his day, or an hour if we have another in the afternoon. Only eight more hours to fill.

I sit at my desk, trying to focus on the list I set myself the day before. Work, admin, a couple of calls, news, and writing. It's a pity it comes in that order, with writing, my new love, at the end. I don't always get to the bottom of my list.

He pops his head in. 'Sorry to interrupt, but if you have five minutes, could you help me print something. I can't get the computer to work. It's so bloody frustrating.' I breath in, the breath rising on a familiar mix of tension and pity. It's 10:36am and it's started. I breathe out, slow and deliberate, to quell my irritation and damp the pain.

'Sure, just give me a minute.'

He stands at my desk, peering over my shoulder. I stare at the screen, fingers hovering over the keys, waiting for him to move on, and as I wait, I feel my jaw clench. 'I said I'd help you in a minute. I'd like to finish something first.' My voice has an edge to it, frustration already slipping through the cracks. It's 10:38am.

I help him print the documents, file them. I delete emails that could lead to him getting scammed again, and leave him sitting at his desk eagerly thumbing through materials he'll spend the next few hours trying to understand. I return to my study to find my place and start again.

My concentration is broken when I hear footsteps in the hall, and I pray that they will move towards the front door rather than my office.

'I've just found this which you might be interested in.' Damn. I close my eyes and breathe.

'What is it?' I ask. The brightness in my voice is entirely fake.

'It's an article in today's paper about that TV host, you know, the one who was arrested. What's his name?'

I don't care, but I pretend I do. I look at the photo. It's Andrew O'Connell whose downfall has been uncomfortably public. He's mentally ill and he's made a right hash of his life, poor bastard. Roughed up his wife, fucked up at work. Drugs. The good life must have got too good. What an idiot.

'Thanks, I'll look at it.' I smile, briefly. 'I'm doing something else right now.' It's a gentle hint.

'You should read it. It's quite interesting.'

'Hmmm,' is my response. He places the article that he has carefully torn out of the paper on top of the pile next to me, and leaves, his slow foot steps shuffle along the boards. I hear his chair squeak. How long will it be before the next interruption?

I'm on the phone when he brings me a cup of tea. I type while I am talking, my phone jammed between my shoulder and my ear. I have no more extremities to use to communicate my appreciation for the tea, and my wish for him to go. He hesitates, then wanders over to the bookshelf and thumbs a couple of books, opens one and asks, 'Is this new?'

I'm mid conversation so I shake my head vigorously both to say 'no it's not new', but also to say, 'please go, you're interrupting.'

'I haven't read this one.'

I glance at the title and know he read it just a few months ago, at my suggestion. He reads lots of books these days, many more than he did when he was the head of a large corporation. Fiction reading wasn't on the agenda then. A page or two, once or twice a week, before he fell asleep with the book splayed against his chest, was the most he managed. Since he retired, he reads more but I wonder how much he comprehends. His answer to 'did you enjoy the book?' is always, 'It was 415 pages long'. That puzzles me. It never occurs to me to take note of how long a book is. When I read the words on the final page, I am so submerged in layers of meaning and poignance building on all the previous pages, so awed by the cleverness of the author. I've never noticed the page number. But he always tells me how long the book is as though getting to the last page is actually the point of the exercise, rather than living the story alongside the characters.

That was the first sign.

'Am I expected to make myself lunch?' My phone call has finished, but I wish it hadn't because I might have missed this last question. My response is disproportionate. I am enraged; boiling.

'You don't have to have lunch at all,' I snap. It's passive aggressive but he doesn't react. He is no longer able to gauge implied meanings.

'Oh.' He puts the book back and wanders down the hall. I feel terrible, like I've kicked a puppy, and immediately I get up to make lunch for us. It's 12:05pm, more like morning tea time, but lunch is getting earlier and earlier. Perhaps that's what happens when lunch is the only event in a day that stretches out until the end.

He takes my suggestion to go for a walk after lunch, while the sun's out. I hope it stays out so that he does too. The sounds of my empty house are a balm for my soul that I crave like a drug.

He's back in time to meet the girls at the bus stop. I am grateful they are still young enough to enjoy being met. I suspect it won't be long before they will cringe, and wish for a father who is still at work when the school bus arrives.

'Will you take the girls to tennis?' he asks me, when they come in the door.

'It's swimming today, and yes, I will.'

'I can take them if you like; give you a bit more time to finish off.'

It's a kind offer, but I refuse. He got lost last time and they missed their lesson. Instead, he tries to help them get ready but just manages to get in the way as they rush around looking for swimmers and towels, thongs, goggles. In a bluster of bags and 'hurry up', we're in the car, just the girls and I, and I breathe again, deeply this time. Their happy chatter fills the space, and for a moment, I am content.

It lasts until we get home.

The Chase blares through the house, broadcasting the fate of hapless contestants. The trivia host feigns remorse when he successfully chases down the contestants, but I'm certain his remuneration is linked to quashing contestant's dreams. It's not the only reason I hate The Chase. I hate all daytime TV; it's for people who have nothing better to do. I used to think quiz shows were light entertainment, but now I know they're designed to help the aged keep their marbles and timed to counteract the sun-downers, that time of day late in the afternoon when cognitive confusion sets in. So the TV is my constant dinner-prep companion in this open planned house. I answer the questions despite my contempt of it, and pour myself a drink.

I insist upon a family dinner every night. It's how I was brought up and parenting experts say it's important. The girls will need all the help they can get, given what lies ahead. They are funny and dramatic and I enjoy their story telling, but more often than not, they are interrupted by a random comment or question, something completely irrelevant to what they are telling me. It happens every day, so I should expect it, and yet, every time, I am surprised that he's not following the conversation. Sometimes I wonder whether he even realises one is taking place, when he interrupts. The sharp raconteur I bantered with for all those years has disappeared. It's another crushing reminder. The pain is deep, but I ignore it and allow exasperation to override it. I remind the whole family that interrupting is rude, knowing the youngest listeners have learned that lesson already. It is their father who has forgotten.

It's finally time and all three go to bed. He kisses his daughters good night, tucks them in and they respond with fierce hugs that almost pull him off his feet. He says good night to me and kisses my cheek. His kiss would land on the lips if I allowed it, but I turn my head. Kisses on the mouth are for lovers. Yet another sign of what has been lost. How many have there been today? I've stopped counting.

The house is silent. This is my time. There are no more demands on me, just late-night hours to write, binge watch, or read. I do it all to escape. Always with a drink in hand–one more than I should have. The one I'll regret when I wake.

The hours tick by and I forget my loneliness. When my vision starts to blur and my eyelids slide like broken sash windows that won't stay open, I go to our room. It's dark and quiet; only slivers of grey slip through small gaps in the shutters. I wait by the door.

A mopoke calls softly, and I am tempted to wake him so he can hear the mournful sound. Instead, I listen for the quiet sighs from the wizened mound tucked beneath layers of blankets to ward off the cold.

Pyjamas are laid out on my pillow, and the covers folded back, like a turndown service in a hotel. Annoyed that he permeates even this, the simple act of getting into bed, I am appalled I am so ungrateful. I don't deserve such love or reverence. My terseness and exasperation should be met with a nasty comment or a rage, but every night it's the same–a delicate and understated memento of his steadfastness. I change in the dark so I don't disturb him, but the darkness hides my shame. Between the cool sheets, freezing and huddled into myself, I can't warm my extremities. Even tucking my legs up and blowing warm breath on my hands isn't enough. A hand slips gently across my waist, and his wiry arm pulls me against his sunken chest as he nestles against me.

The warmth of his body seeps through my back, and his hand, clasped over mine, is silken and untroubled. Clenched fists soften and tension drains from my limbs as I let go of the armour I have built to protect myself.

We are back at the beginning, when words won my heart, but now they warn me. The poems from the collection he gave me, the ones at the back that I used to ignore, poems of Love Lost and Love Remembered speak to soul. They warn me to hold the heart that holds mine gently, for it may soon be gone.

Heart/Broken
Taryn Donohue

My brother and I, we grew up rough. An absent father led to a broken mother, and we all know how that goes. Trouble in school. Trouble in life. But we always had each other and the only person who understood our particular brand of childhood is him.

I don't remember the first time we met Amy Manning. This is not that kind of love story. Hell, maybe it's not a love story at all. But by the time we started high school, it was always the three of us. Amy, Aaron and me. Loitering at the shops after school buying milkshakes, hanging at the skate park on weekends, sneaking smokes behind the garden shed out the back of our place. From the get go, I was conscious of her in a way that I didn't even understand. I could tell you where she was standing in any room without even looking around. Aaron named it before I could, in only the way older brothers do. I denied it, of course. If you ask me now, I will deny it still.

Don't get me wrong. Amy wasn't like us. Not at all. Nice house, clean clothes, packed lunches. Mr Manning drove her to school every day.

Her mother wasn't at home on the couch escaping into Days of Our Lives with a bottle of cheap bourbon glued to her hand. And yet, here we are, the three of us. It's not a love triangle. It's a more messed up geometry of love than that.

Amy presses her eyes closed against the waves of pain. He said he'd be back. Shit. Please God tell me he hasn't done a runner again.

She grimaces and grabs my hand, squeezing it hard before letting out a cry. It's loud, guttural and almost inhuman. The contraction peaks and passes, and she sags back against the bed.

'Dan, I can't...'

Tears slip down her face and I want to take her pain away. I also want to find my brother and drag him in here by this hair. But it's too late. I can't let her do this alone.

'Listen to me, Amy. You can do this. You can do anything.'

We always looked out for Aaron even though he's a few years older than us. He tried so hard not to be our father, not to be our mother. But one way or another, it crept in. First with the drink, then with drugs. Then with harder drugs. The school counsellor told him it only makes things worse, but it was hard for Aaron to untangle everything, to find the beginning of the thread. Did it start when our father left, or when his father left him? Or did it start in that cold shower room at school, when everyone else had gone home for the day?

I don't know what was worse: watching my brother crumble, or the stone weight of guilt that formed in my stomach and stayed there. Without ever speaking a word, Amy and I committed ourselves to augment and sustain him, to cover his nakedness with our love. So even though she had once kissed me, under the shade of a pale cherry blossom coming into full bloom, from that moment on, she devoted herself to him. I'm not saying they wouldn't have ended up together if not for what happened. It's impossible now to untwine love and longing from the shame, and pain, and guilt. Maybe it could have been different between me and her, would have been different, if either of us had been free to choose. But we weren't free. We weren't ever free.

She's been labouring for hours, and she is magnificent and primal and fierce. She breathes and grimaces and breathes again. I rub gentle circles on her back, and she gives a low moan and sets her face doggedly against the pain and keeps going. I expect nothing less. She has always been stubborn.

The midwife says she can see the head, and I sit behind her, supporting her. Then little Jay is born. Right before my eyes, he makes his way into the world, screaming the walls down, curlew-like, and red raw.

Amy weeps, an intermingling of happy and sad tears. She is holding her son, but Aaron is not here.

Soon she lies heavy-armed, hardly able to circle Jay, as he rests skin to skin on her bare breasts. The nurse drapes a warmed blanket over them both and the doctor, still fussing around, asks me if I want to cut the cord. I shake my head. I should tell him I am not the father.

Jay grows silent, and blue tinges his lips. A nurse sweeps him up and Amy cries out, reaching for her son.

'What's going on?' I yell, too loudly.

You would think that in a small, coastal town, it would be worse. The rumours, the innuendo. Gossip runs like fire here, everyone knows everyone else's business. And they knew, but instead of blowing up into a blaze of indignation, it dwindled to a spot fire, and finally a pile of ash. In a powerful act of mass hypnosis, they all decided to un-remember what happened. It was easier that way. The tide of dreadful knowing had crashed in on them, and instead of swimming against it, they let the wave sweep over them while they lay, still and safe, in the silence, at the bottom of the ocean.

Trust me, I understand why they chose to drown instead of facing it. Hell, I wanted to do that too. And Aaron, he certainly tried hard to drown himself–booze, pills, and even the sharp edge of a kitchen knife.

But it was still there, in every moment of every day. It took up one of the cracked leather stools in the corner of the milk bar, it slunk in through the school library doors, it crouched in the corner of mine and Aaron's bedroom. He would wake in the night, his sheets soaked in sweat and urine, screaming in the darkness. As he turned over to sleep again, I would lay there, silent and wakeful, and swear that I could hear his broken heart, tapping out its fragmented rhythm. Tump-tump, tump-tump, tump-clank. Sometimes I would hold my breath, listening, ready to leap from the bottom bunk and start compressions on my brother's chest, in case the rhythm ever completely stopped. I knew it was up to me to resurrect him, to keep him bodily alive.

'What the hell is going on?' I know I am shouting too loudly, again, but I don't care.

No-one answers me as the grim moments pass. They fuss over Jay's little body. Amy cries out for her son, pushing my hands away as I try to prevent her leaving the bed.

'Someone answer me!' I am wild with panic.

Jay's cry rings out again, strong and clear, and I feel the mood of the room settle and ebb. They bring him back to us, naked, squirming and reassuringly pink.

'He's fine,' the nurse says as she nestles him on Amy's chest again. 'Just a bit of mucous in his airways, all cleared up now.'

Jay nuzzles his mother, and opens his dark, watchful eyes. Amy's face is wet with sweat and tears as she looks at me. I take her hand and lean over, pressing a soft kiss to her forehead. If ever I dreamt of this moment, long ago, when we were all still kids, she looked just like this. A damp, pale angel as I cradled her and our newborn son in my arms. In my dream, there was no shadow of the past on her face.

'He's so perfect, Dan. Look at him.' And I am looking. Always.

Our town had a short memory for what happened to Aaron, but a long one for all the things he did trying to find his own place of forgetting.

He had no more control over it than any of the other shit that happened in our lives, but some how he was expected to assimilate it, carry the weight of it, walk on, as if he hadn't had his legs amputated below the knees.

It wasn't enough to let him be. They found ways to punish him over, and over again. Leaving school? Don't think you can come here for an apprenticeship. You might be a functional alcoholic, but you're still a drunk. Why are you looking at my son like that, you bloody pervert?

The mantle of it settled over us like a fine spider's web, sticky, and with a hidden strength. Tarred by association, and a refusal to abandon him to the miry darkness of the past, Amy and I were also cast out. But she was the eternal optimist, driving us forward. So, we made our own way, setting up a little photography business, selling landscapes and beach shots.

Amy always had a camera in her hand. A cheap little Kodak at first, then a better one, with a fancy detachable lens and manual settings, and finally a beautiful, sleek Leica that we drove to Sydney to pick up. She took it everywhere with her, and everywhere she found beauty. Shorelines and sunsets became ethereal under her fingers. Aaron and I knew shit about photography, but I took a crash course on making websites and he built the custom frames, carefully stretching the printed canvas images over the edges, nailing and finishing the final products. We went to all the festivals and fetes, mainly selling to tourists and eventually online.

It wasn't much, but it was enough. We lived cheap for the most part. But Aaron was still drinking, and he would disappear, sometimes into his own head, with that rapt look in his eyes, and sometimes physically, for weeks at a stretch. Those days were long, and Amy would sit on the veranda, hugging her knees and staring out at the road, like she could make him come home just by sheer force of her will. Hell, for all I know it worked, because he always turned up eventually, ducking his head apologetically, tight-lipped about where he had been.

They never fought, not openly, not in front of me. But it was like she was one of the porcelain figurines on the mantel in my mother's house, and I was always waiting for him to carelessly knock her off at the same time as I willed him to take her in his arms and cradle her. The months turned into years, and there was never anyone else. My longing for her never abated, but nor did my hope of seeing Aaron made whole, at peace. It was like being constantly torn in different directions that led to the same terminus. A war waged within myself, an intractable paradox, beyond my ability to resolve.

When Aaron finally shows up at the hospital, hours after Jay's birth, Amy is passed out, her head lolling on the pillow, the baby tucked in beside her. I am perched on the edge of the chair by the bed, watching.

'Where the hell have you been?'

He stands at the end of the bed, gazing silently at his sleeping wife and newborn son. He raises his eyes mechanically to the sound of my voice.

'A bus crashed near Goulburn. Completely blocked the roads.'

There is sincerity in his eyes, but alcohol on his breath. For Amy and Jay's sake, I desperately want to believe that he would not have missed his own son's birth because he was holed up in a bar on the highway in the middle of the day.

'How is she?' He asks, returning his gaze to her.

'She'll be fine,' I say, trying not to think about the mess of bloodied sheets and how long they spent stitching her up, while drugged to the eyeballs, she blissfully cooed over her baby.

'Were you here for it? The birth and all?'

'Yeah, I was here.' Aaron nods but doesn't look at me. He leans over the bed and gently lifts Jay into his arms. Jay snuffles loudly and when Aaron holds him close to his chest, for a second, I see our father in the only photo we still have of him, the one at the hospital the day Aaron was born. Just like dad, he looks proud and panicked.

Amy stirs and opens her eyes. 'Aaron,' she breathes. He sinks to the bed beside her. 'It's a boy Aaron, it's Jay,' she says, reaching out to touch her baby's cheek. Aaron leans in to kiss his wife and I look away.

Aaron and Amy got married at the beach on a hot summer's day with the sea breeze coming in. She was barefoot with a garland of flowers on her head and a creamy lace dress draped over her already-swollen belly. Aaron wore an open-collared shirt that I ironed for him that morning. Mum pulled herself together for the occasion, teetering across the sand in platform red heels and a too-tight dress. There was the celebrant, me, and Amy's sister, Louise, who came down from Sydney. I smiled tightly as they murmured their promises and signed the legal papers.

After the ceremony, we retreated to a local place for a few drinks and dinner. Louise leaned across the table and whispered, 'You're a good bloke, supporting him this way, supporting them.' She winked at me as she nodded in my brother's direction. I shrugged and watched Aaron thread his way through the crowd towards the bar. It was a low threshold for being a good bloke, as far as things go. Turn up at your brother's wedding and keep your bloody mouth shut about your long-held feelings for his almost-wife. Truth is, no other option made sense. I had never loved anyone else except for those two, now almost three.

Amy gets the all clear to leave hospital the day after the birth and it feels too soon but what do I know? She dresses Jay in a white jumpsuit and tucks a tiny knitted beanie over his head. Aaron says he will get the car. After fifteen minutes, I go to the carpark, my eyes roving along the rows, desperately hoping I'll see the blue sedan with a baby capsule in the back. I walk up and down for another fifteeen minutes. When I lift my eyes, Amy is standing at the hospital door, cradling the baby in one arm and holding her bag with the other, her face resigned.

We take the bus home and neither of us speaks about Aaron at all. What is left to say that could make a difference? There's no point acknowledging he screwed up. Again. I am here to sort things out. Again. Is that why he goes? Or is that why he can't stay?

I can't untangle the thread any more than Aaron can. If I'm honest, I stopped even trying a long time ago. In that shower room at school, a promise was broken that should never have to be made. Aaron never would say how many times it happened, not even after the police got involved. But those details don't even count, don't even matter now, because what's done is done. And under that repulsive fluorescent light, Aaron was undone and he's been undone ever since.

Amy's mum still visits her dad once or twice a year, wherever he is holed up now. Magistrate sentenced him two years and he was out on probation orders after eighteen months. She left town, so they didn't get to shit on her the way they did Aaron and us. I don't know if she'll ever meet Jay. We never knew how much she knew, if there were others before Aaron, whether she even told the whole truth in the end. That was harder for Amy than what her father had done. Did her mother know and never say? Maybe others had kept silent too? I can't live in those questions every day, can't dwell there, or else I want to scratch my brains out.

Jay will be one-year-old next weekend. He started walking around eleven months old and now he's nearly running. We scramble to keep up, chasing his little bum all over the house.

I don't know what else to tell you. The sins of the father and all that. It's only because of Amy I know that we aren't doomed to repeat the past. Not entirely. She's too hopeful to ever become our mother. Also, she hates bourbon.

She's taught Jay to call me Dan but it sounds like 'dad' the way his baby lips and mouth from the word. One day his father will walk through our front door, pulled back to us by gravity itself. We, the gawping black hole of the past and the future. And I'll try to hate him, and Amy will too. But the urge to forgive, to mend, will be too strong. The unvoiced promise we made all those years ago will take shape again and bind us back together in a way that we can never understand or escape. We will shepherd little Jay into this contract too, lovingly, and with faith.

Like all the other dumb punters in this world, there are so many things I would change if we could undo the past, rewrite the script. But we can't go back. We can never go back.

So, I'll scrape out whatever happiness I can from the relative position of our figures in this strange geometry of love. You see, however much it hurts, it is the only measure of the earth as I know it, the thing that gives the world distance, shape and size. This convergence we return to again, and again, is the axiom of my life. It is broken and imperfect, as choppy as the sea before a storm, the waves churning over each other, rising to a crescendo before plummeting down again. But it will abide with us always, the unerring map of our heart.

Too Many Mothers
Laura Kelly

It was at Emily's funeral that I first felt her baby kick inside me. And with that churning flutter, I knew deep in my bones that I would do anything I could to keep it. To keep her.

The smell of the incense and the lilies were making the saliva pool at the back of my mouth and I felt the familiar numbness spread across my upper back as nausea rose. I closed my eyes and took a deep breath, but my face was covered in too much mucous, too many tears. All I could taste was salt. When I looked up I could see Emily's mother-in-law clutching Nick's shoulder as they both shook silently in the row ahead of me. Nick seemed older than his mother, frail and withered in his suit. His neck was red and thin. Somehow Clemmie's frosted silver bob was as immaculate as always. But something was wrong with the size of them. Nick had always been able to fold Emily into the crook of his arm, but now he looked smaller than I remembered.

Tears flowed down my neck and I did nothing to staunch them. I tried to concentrate on the feel of my toes in my shoes.

None of the service felt like Emily. None of it. Not the tasteful walnut casket or the monstrous crucifix looming over proceedings, or the faux-reverent purple-robed father who intoned at the front. Where was she in all of this? Hadn't she joked about a cardboard box and a forest where we all had to bring a spade and sing spirituals while we drank mojitos? We'd imagined being doddering old ladies together, only dying once we'd become well and truly sick of ourselves.

She'd made it sound fun when we'd dreamed up our funerals together, just the way we'd planned for our holidays and our boyfriends and our weddings and our babies. All adventure, all warmth, all shimmer. But instead there was just…this. Years had passed in the days since the accident, and her absence sat inside me and upon me.

It was never meant to be my egg. We'd always planned for it to be Em and Nick's baby. I'd just carry it for them. We knew I could; I'd had a good pregnancy. Completed my family. Completed my marriage. Completely fucked up my chances at another. But I knew I could do this for her, and I hadn't waited for her to ask. I'd already been there for every IVF cycle, every cursed period, every miscarriage, every bit of bad news about egg retrieval and severe endometriosis and the surgeries that had ended the charade that it was going to happen for her.

I knew the hollowness of her grief, the shape of her rage, the effort it took to bring lightness to her face when all she felt was failure and emptiness every time it went wrong. She was deep down underground when everyone else was walking on the surface, and no one was noticing how far under she was, screaming inside her subterranean cavern. Who was ever going to bring her out? It couldn't be Nick. He was the same coin, but stuck on the other side, unable to reach her.

I knew it could be me. I could give her this. I wanted to. So I'd offered to carry a baby for them. Nick's sperm. My egg. My womb. Their baby.

Emily's baby.

I shifted in the wooden pew and felt Grace by my side, composed and desperately young with her bowl cut and long earrings and black turtleneck. It was her first big loss, her favourite Aunty Em, and the stoic set of her shoulders hurt my heart. In front of me, I watched Nick. I could see the faded acne scars of his adolescence dappled across the back of his neck. I remembered him from back then, a sudden flash of the lean, shy debater who had doted on Emily, who had loved her calmly and wholeheartedly from the start. She'd joked about him and she'd teased him a little and then she'd fallen in love with him. He'd been there with us ever since. He was clever and funny and he loved Emily for exactly who she was. I'd envied them that. The way they just loved each other without wanting to change one another. Nick was a good man. One of the best. But I knew I couldn't give him this baby anymore.

It wasn't Nick's fault. He'd have been a wonderful dad if Emily had been at his side. But I could already see him folding back into childhood under the weight of his grief, handing over control of Em's funeral to his mum and his sisters like they'd know best. But how could they know best how to honour Emily? How could they know better than him? Who the fuck had ordered the lilies for the casket? Em had hated lilies, always.

It would be the same with the baby. I knew men, and I knew babies. He wasn't going to be up to the task. He'd want to do it, of course. For Emily. But he had no idea what he was getting himself into. I remembered with full bodily force the shock of Grace's early days and the deadening fatigue and anxiety. The crushing weight of it all, and the insanity of the love. How awful and exhilarating it was, how like a drug-fuelled nightmare.

How could he do any of that without Emily? At first he'd just get his mother to help. Mind the baby. Help around the house. Clemmie and the girls. Always helpful, always on hand. He'd try and involve me, of course. He'd want to do what was right. But Clemmie would take over and it would be nothing like what Emily had planned. It would be the exact opposite of what she'd have wanted. It would be sleep training and don't make a rod for your own back and spoil her now and you'll never hear the end of it. It would be emotional whack-a-mole; squash down every cry, every tantrum, every defiant question. How Nick had escaped so unscathed from that family had remained a mystery for the ages, and Em had joked about it often. Even Nick knew she did. I couldn't just hand Emily's baby over to Clemmie for fuck's sake, it would feel like delivering a sacrificial morsel to a wolf.

My blood pulsed slow and heavy as I reached out for Grace's hand. She was my baby, and yet she was a grown woman now. Older than I had been when I'd birthed her. I could feel the uncertainty and shock vibrating off her, and all I could do was hold on. She didn't know how to lose someone she loved, not this soon. She needed me. She didn't need any more chaos. She needed her mother.

And besides, there was no way I could have this baby on my own. Nick would never just hand her over, and I was struggling to keep this family afloat as it was. But nevertheless, my knowledge sat inside me. Alongside the baby and her fluttering kicks.

I had to have this baby and do it Emily's way. I was the only one that could.

Never before had pregnant women bothered me, but today I could barely look at them. The waiting room was full of them; radiant, full of light, laughing with partners and absent-mindedly stroking their bellies. I was like their inversion, heavy and bloated and full to the bursting with nothingness.

I'd waited three weeks since the funeral, telling myself over and again that the 20 week scan would give him some time to process the funeral, to realise how much things had changed. To realise that she wasn't here anymore, that we couldn't go on as planned.

Last time I was in this waiting room, Emily was next to me. Linking her arm through mine, leaning on my shoulder like a conspirator as we talked about where to buy cloth nappies from. She was reading about Reggio Emilio and wanted to set up a nursery to encourage the baby's independence and exploration. I'd wanted to shield her from her own excitement, but I couldn't. She was confident in a way she'd never been with her own pregnancies.

I pushed down the memories of the times before that, in this room and others; the times when I'd been at her side for the scans that showed no heartbeat, for the consultations with terse doctors who told her that her body was failing to respond to treatment. For the dosages to take home and insert so she could quietly bleed away her hope, again. I knew these rooms were brutal for her in a way I couldn't quite fathom, and that somehow she'd managed to bring something bright and hard to the surface to get through it all.

Now the sight of these ripe women and their doting partners filled me with a kind of childish rage, and I told myself it was on her behalf. How dare they do this without all the extra baggage to carry? Where the fuck was their dead friend and their ethical conundrum? I hated that our daughter was now stewing in grief and anger, instead of sur-rounded by love and softness.

I felt the weight of my decision in my chest, constricting my breath-ing and bringing a deadening kind of stillness. Still like concrete, not like peace. The taste of the Buscopan was making everything worse; maybe even the reflux itself.

Where the hell is Nick? Surely he can't be late to this.

Last time there'd been Emily's face when they showed us the heart-beat of our little blob. Nick had been interstate for work. It was just us. Everything was right there on Emily's face; the joy, the memories of the tiny babies she'd never quite met. The envy and the awe.

'You're going to be a warrior woman,' she said. Her words held grief and love and anger and hope.

Now there were just duck-egg blue walls and shitty posters about lis-teria and IVF. I felt the baby flutter. A nurse in dark blue scrubs called my name, holding a clipboard and smiling warmly.

'Fiona Stewart.'

It's time. Time to see you again little one.

I didn't know whether I was talking to Emily or the baby.

I was on the table getting sticky gel squirted on my lower belly when Nick arrived. I felt a little fizz of excitement as the sonographer placed the scanner near my right hip and started digging down and sideways into my bloated abdomen.

Nick sat down next to me and I watched the screen for a beat longer than I needed to. I didn't want to look at him. I could feel the heaviness he carried. It was like a sickness, and it reminded me of my own. I didn't want our sickness near the baby.

He reached out for my shoulder and squeezed it. It made me want to weep, just feeling his familiarity and what I had to tell him.

Nick reached for my hand and his sadness flowed into me as our palms pressed together. It took my breath away, what we were carrying inside. Tears sat behind my eyes and I felt the heaviness of Emily's absence on my shoulders, curling my chin to my chest.

'There it is,' the sonographer said. She had sculpted eyebrows and shimmering bronzed cheeks above her black face mask. She was kind and a little bit coarse, despite the neatness of her appearance.

She clicked to expand the image and I could make out a huge head and a tiny curled body.

'That's a strong little heartbeat. Finally got her. That's your little one right there.'

She didn't mean my little one. She meant 'ours.' Nick's and mine. Our little one. Emily's baby was ours.

'Nick. I don't think…' I began, but I couldn't finish it. My throat was too thick with the tears I was holding in. I hated seeing how naked he looked, his elation shining through his pallor.

I don't think I can go through with this. I can't give you this baby.

'I don't think I can believe it either. It's like she's here with us,' said Nick, tears falling silently down his cheeks. He took a long jagged breath, and smiled a little.

How could I tell him now?

'It's Emily's little girl. Finally. Our bubs. Hello little one,' he said softly. He wanted her too. As badly as I did.

♥ ♥ ♥

'I want to say thank you Fee. I know it hasn't been easy on you, and I know how much you and Emily meant to each other. I can only imagine what it's like going through this while you're looking after Grace. You were always a good friend to Em. To us.'

Something about the weird formality of this little speech made my teeth come together tightly as I listened.

'I just know how much this meant to Em. How much she wanted to be a mum...' He rolled his lips inwards quickly, giving himself a moment to pause.

'How thankful she was. I want you to know that if you would like to be a part of it, you know, bringing up this baby, I am open to that. I've already started talking to Mum and Bonnie and Tess, about how we're going to juggle it. I'll probably get the first month or two off, and Mum's thinking she'll move in. Maybe for the first year or so. Bonnie can too, for a bit. She's even started looking at day-care centres for me in the city.'

My blood froze. The ultrasound transducer was pressing right on my bladder and the sonographer was clicking and muttering apologies as she stared at her screen.

'I can't do it Nick.'

'What? Be involved?'

'I can't carry this baby for you to bring up with your mum. Can you imagine what Em would say if Clemmie was raising this baby?'

I saw his spine straighten, eyes narrow. Head to the side. Nick was becoming a debater again.

'What do you mean exactly?' His voice was tight.

A woman laughed loudly out in the waiting room. The sonographer kept quietly digging, quietly clicking her screen.

'I mean this is not just your baby Nick. This is my body going through this. My heart. I love this baby, too. It's Em's daughter, but she's mine too. Especially now. And I know she's yours as well. But I did this for Em. For you both, together. And it's changed. It's changed too much. And now that I can feel her kicking...'

I took a deep breath.

'I'm her mother. It's just so clear to me now that this is my little girl too. And that it's my job to bring her up, now that her other mum won't be here.'

'So wait. What exactly are you proposing Fee? Are you just planning on taking the baby?'

'Not taking her. Just not…giving her up. I want to be her mother.'

Nick knitted his dark eyebrows together and looked off to the side of my face. He was trying to compute what I was saying.

'Hold on. I know what this is. Remember the counselling sessions? Back at the start. It's totally normal for a surrogate to feel apprehensive sometimes. It's a huge thing, the sacrifice you're making. We all understand that. The counsellor said that grief and jealousy are completely normal. But it passes as the hormones settle.'

I'm not a fucking incubator. I'm her mother. Her other mother.

'I thought you wanted to do this for us,' he said quietly.

'For Emily.'

'But you offered this to us Fiona. You offered. You know you can't just take that back.' He looked down at his hands and his voice became careful.

'We signed a contract.'

'I'm not a fucking stranger Nick, and it's not about my hormones. I'm saying I can't just give this baby up when she's born. Not to you. Not to anybody. I'm so sorry. I want to be able to but I can't. I know what Emily wanted, and it wasn't this. It wasn't you and your mum, and your sisters and day-care in the city. It just wasn't.'

'Where do I fit in then?'

'I know how much you've wanted to be a dad. But it's not the same.'
'Not the same for fathers? We can't feel what you feel?'

I hesitated. I noticed his knuckles were white, gripping his chair. He looked so scared and small. I spoke softly this time. I looked at the screen, the white sheet over my legs. I took a breath.

'I want to be able to raise this child in a way that Emily would have wanted. And in a way that I know is best. I want to be her mother. I am her mother. I know babies Nick, I know how to do this. I know that I can.'

'And you think I can't?'

'I think you are swallowed up by grief right now. I think you want a project to focus on and I think you hope this will bring Emily back. But a baby's not a project Nick.'

'I never said it was. You've got some fucking crazy idea that I can't love her the way you can, that I want to back out of it all.'

'I think you want to stick to the original plan because you are a good man. You want to do what's right. You want to honour Emily and you don't want to leave me in the shit. I get it. And I know you want to be a dad. But like this? You've got no idea what bringing up a baby–a child– really involves. It's a lot, on your own. And I don't think you can do it like this. Not properly.'

Nick's silence stretched around the room, blanketing everything. The sonographer removed the transducer and handed me some paper towel to wipe myself clean. Her fingernails were a sickly peach colour, and they were weirdly thick and a little too long. How did she get anything done with them? She stood and left the room without a word.

'So you want me to lose my wife first and then my child? That's the plan? To sign a contract and get our hopes up and then back out now that I've lost everything.'

His face was hard again. I could imagine him in a courtroom. I knew there was someone good under that angry shell, but I couldn't remember that well enough not to hate him in that moment. I knew what I was doing was awful for him, but I also knew it was right.

'I know it's not going to be easy. But I can make it work. I know I've done a good job with my own kid. Em knew that. I booked the first five months off work after the birth anyway, to help Em out. I've got a permanent position at the library, with flexible hours. Long service leave coming up. I'm a good mum. The type of mum Emily would have wanted. I've worked with kids for fourteen years. And I love this baby.'

'You say you're going to love it as though you think I can't.'

'Her.' I said quietly. 'I already do.'

'Yeah, yes. Her. She's my child as well Fee.'

'Mine too.'

'You can't just take this away from me. Don't you see that?'

'But don't you see Nick? Things have changed. So much. And we could never have known it would be like this. We were both willing to do anything for Em. Anything. But she's gone. Now it's just thinking about this little person who's going to arrive.'

'So you think the best thing for this child is being raised by a single mother with a university drop out still living at home. You know Grace has enough issues as it is. You're still drowning in the debts from how many different schools?'

I didn't rise to the bait.

'I don't think any of the options are good. There's nothing about this that's turning out how we'd hoped. How she'd hoped.'

'You say it like you know her better than I do. Knew her.'

A sob escaped from him and I said nothing. Emily only lived in the past tense now.

'Maybe we can split the custody. We could set up both our houses, do one week on, one week off?' His eyes were pleading.

Are you insane? Traipsing a newborn baby across town, ripping her away from her mother for half the time?

'I can't do it Nick. Without Emily. I can't just become a mother who gives up my child into a situation that I can't live with. It feels too wrong.'

He looked so crestfallen I wondered if I could take it back. But I knew I couldn't.

'Having kids turns you inside out and take you right to the edges of yourself Nick. I don't think you can do it.'

I took a long, shallow breath. My ribs felt tight. I could feel how heavy my legs were, and how much I needed to pee.

Nick sighed. Nodded.

Something in him softened at the same time I started to think of all the reasons that perhaps I was wrong. The weird hetero sexist assumption that the child needed her mother more than she needed her father. The financial stress I was already under. The worries about what to do once I had to go back to juggling work and baby, the way I had with Grace. The panic of it all, and the loneliness.

Nick spoke slowly, looking at the ground. 'I can take time off, when the baby's born. As much as I need to. I can work from home, go down to part-time hours. I want to be a part of this.'

When he said it, I felt relief and the full force of our shared desolation. Nick looked at me then, leaking tears and reaching for my hand.

His face. My god, his face. I'd broken something, and I couldn't yet see the path out of it.

It wasn't until a pre-natal yoga class nearly two months later that I first felt something loosen. Every day of the pregnancy had been murky with nausea and the shock of not doing it with Emily. I hadn't signed up for this alone, and the pressure felt flattening. Grace was quietly getting on with applying for part-time jobs, but I could never tell what she was thinking anymore. She'd drawn into herself, and I couldn't reach her. She'd been spending more time at her Dad's and I didn't even have the energy to ask her about it.

Had I done enough for Grace when she was younger? Had I been a good mum? Was I doing enough now that she was grown? Was anything a mother did ever enough? I'd have to find my way back to her.

I lay on my side holding a bolster between my legs, my stomach distended and unwieldy atop two folded grey blankets. The instructor placed more heavy blankets on top of me and pressed a small silky wheat pillow to my eyes.

As soon as the lights were down the tears came, soaking the little lavender pillow and dribbling down into my ear. The sadness was there, but the desperation wasn't. I was still like an empty bag, full to the bursting with nothingness. And somehow, underneath the nothingness, an overwhelming ache. It coated all it touched with its beautiful, terrible knowledge of everything ending, always.

I was still tuned in to Radio Emily every time I paused. She still ran on loops through my mind, tucking her feet up under her on the couch, fluffy house socks on, wine in hand. Laughing and frowning during cosy British mysteries. Emily Blake: green eyes, stealthy grin, steady kindness.

My body shook, but I felt strangely calm as the tears kept coming. Nothing really seemed more or less healed than it had three months ago.

But something had shifted. Just a little. The fear wasn't sitting underneath everything quite as much now. I could remember Emily and I could feel the baby inside, both at once. And I knew I could do it. But not alone.

I smelled the white sage of the studio and half listened to the ringing music bowl as the instructor chanted. I felt baby fluttering and I loved her fiercely and without words.

Nick had agreed to fortnightly counselling sessions with a surrogacy expert. We talked about grief and co-parenting and attachment theory. Sometimes we just sat on the beige couch together and wept. Nobody knew my pain the way Nick did. Once we had both had Emily. Now we only had each other, bound by grief and by the child we had created together.

I'd found my way back to laughing with him again, to liking him. I'd found my way back to seeing that Emily would want him doing everything he could to be her baby's father. The savage protectiveness I felt had managed to become just a little more elastic. Not enough to include Clemmie yet, but maybe just enough to bind this child with the people who could love her the way her mother would have done.

And the truth was, the nightmares had begun by then. The choking gasp to wakefulness after a vivid hallucination of being trapped in bed with a dead baby down at my feet. I would search and search for her, but she was impossible to find under the covers and there was no-one to help me. I could almost feel the coldness of her silky skin, but I could never find her. There were different versions, always with me alone and wondering how to bear the weight of my obligation and my love.

The night visions merged with memories; memories I had held back ever since Emily had died. Memories of the darkness inside my mother-love, the moments that had frightened me with Grace that I'd never wanted to repeat again. The long afternoons of being trapped with a screaming baby, the fractured sleep, the lashing out at anyone who tried to help. The constant assault on my nervous system, and the shame I'd felt when once again I hadn't been the mother I had hoped to be. The claustrophobia and the addiction.

So much of it had been alone, with Grace. I was still two years away from meeting Emily when I'd had her. I'd only been eighteen, and Grace's father hadn't had any idea of what had hit us. I'd moved back in with my mother, and he wisely hadn't yet followed. Something seismic had overtaken me immediately when Grace was born, and he'd remained back in our other reality, still as untouched and free as a child himself. I'd envied him his sovereignty, and I'd pitied him. I dove back down into the well of my sticky devotion to Grace, and I did not come up for air.

But I couldn't do it again like that, and I was old enough now to know it.

Tomorrow Nick was looking for a rental nearby. There was something on the next cul-de-sac over from mine. Nothing was certain about how we were going to do it. It was going to be untidy and painful and chaotic, and I still wasn't sure what was right. We were both damaged, irreparably, and we were also strangely luminous with the love we'd lost. It was tremulous and overflowing. We wanted it to go somewhere, to touch something new. Someone new.

Grief was going to wrap itself around everything we did, and this baby's other mother would be a ghost shaped by our memories. But it was the only way.

I pressed on the lavender bag that sat over my wet eyes, pushing down hard. Beneath my eyelids I could see a deep green, dotted with bright emerald flecks. The colour of the heart chakra. I took a shallow, shaky breath. I let the air in, held it a moment and sighed it out. I felt cocooned there, wrapped in blankets and surrounded by the quiet breathing of the other waiting mothers.

I knew I needed to be in communion with others to bring me back to myself enough to be a mother. The enormity of it was overwhelming. To get one child close to adulthood and then to start again. I didn't know if I was strong enough, but I knew that isolation and retreat would defeat me.

And that would never have been Emily's way. She would have had a house full of laughter and chaos, a rotating door of visiting aunties and new friends from the local playgroup, and old friends from work. She would have avoided the loneliness as best she could by reaching out. By loving outwards as well as surrendering to the gravitational pull of loving the baby. And she would have had Nick. He would have been there loving her through it all, even the worst of it. He would have seen her struggles and he would have done what he could do to make it all lighter.

And Emily would have had me. She would always have let me in, no matter how dark it got. She always had.

So it was settled. We would simply have to find a way to create something together.

A messy, painful, terribly sad family, but a family nonetheless: Nick and Emily and the baby and Grace and I. Ghosts and grief and too many mothers, and love enough to make do.

Dead weight
Patrick Boxall

The empty seat is one of the few positives to have come from Liam's suicide. It's a grim reminder, sure, but having adjusted to the sight of an empty 18B, Cal and Danny–Liam's best friends–can't help but feel like they've hit the jackpot. They stretch out and enjoy the extra leg room; request a hot meal for their friend, whom they say is in the bathroom; and because of the space between them, they're able to keep their belongings within arm's reach for the duration of their long-haul flight to London.

They try to avoid talking about Liam. A 32-hour journey across the world is taxing enough without having to unpack the emotional impact of losing a friend, but that said, both Cal and Danny can appreciate how much easier the journey would've been had they remembered to cancel Liam's ticket in the time that has passed since his death.

Ah well.

Shit happens.

Etc.

They try to avoid talking about Liam, but Cal can't help himself. He manages to keep his mouth shut until the plane is somewhere over Indonesia, but the words rise in his throat alongside the waxen sausages and rubbery eggs the airline considers a light British breakfast. He cracks. Turns to Danny and says, 'I wish Liam was here. He would've loved this.'

'Yeah,' says Danny.

'I mean, the old Liam would've loved this. Before, you know, he…before he…back when he was happier, yeah?'

'Yeah.'

'Do you think we're doing the right thing? By going away?'

Danny frowns. 'What?'

'Like, is it disrespectful? To Liam? Is it too soon?'

'Liam's dead. It can't be disrespectful.'

'It might look weird though,' persists Cal. 'To everyone at home, I mean. Us going on holiday so soon. Has anyone messaged you?' He asks because people have been messaging him, asking what the fuck is wrong with him. Who flies to Europe a fortnight after their best friend tops themselves?

'Nah,' lies Danny. 'I haven't heard shit. Besides, Liam is supposed to be with us. We're honouring him. This is what he would've wanted.'

'How can you know that?'

'Know what?'

'That it's what he would've wanted.'

'I just do.'

Cal wants to believe Danny. He wants to believe him so badly, but he can't be sure because Liam stopped telling Cal what he wanted a long time ago. In the rare moments Liam did seem to open up, the conversation always came back to two words: I'm okay.

Cal glances sideways at Danny but his friend is staring straight ahead, moving a plastic glass of beer to his lips, the tray table, back to his lips. Froth clings to his bristly blonde moustache. He wipes it away with a muscular forearm. Cal is grateful for Danny's strength, his toughness. He trusts Danny when he says that everything will be okay.

Everything's okay, thinks Cal.

We're honouring Liam's memory.

This is what he would've wanted.

I'm a good friend.

For now, he buries thoughts of Liam beneath crumbs of complimentary crackers, which pile up in the spot where Liam's bony arse should be sitting. He and Danny take turns brushing them to the ground.

Out of sight.

Out of mind.

Cal is in 18A–the window seat–and as the plane passes over what he thinks is Vietnam, he attempts, unsuccessfully, to get a handle on his emotions. Not because of Liam; rather, he's watching Star Wars and a giant space laser has wiped out the planet Jedha and all its inhabitants. Though Cal has as much experience with interplanetary warfare as he does with processing grief, something about the scene hits him where it hurts.

But that's what happens on planes, right?

Like, a heightened state of emotion or something. As if each passenger's feelings escape and mingle in the recycled air before being inhaled by the collective. A viral load of vulnerability, a potent cocktail of excitement, of possibility.

Cal wipes his eyes and glances, again, to his left. He sees that Danny, in 18C, is having no issue keeping a lid on things. Instead of watching a movie, he's pulled up the in-flight messaging system and is typing away to the passenger in 13F. Cal strains his neck to look over the rows but can't make anything out in the dimmed cabin. He leans over and taps Danny on the shoulder. Asks him what he's doing.

'I'm talking to that blonde girl from the food court,' says Danny.

'The one with her parents?'

'Yep.'

'How do you know where she's sitting? And how do you know if she's eighteen?'

'I don't know if she's eighteen. But I do know that she's five rows ahead of us, three seats across, and pretty quick on the reply.'

'Dude. No.'

'It's harmless,' says Danny, pointing at his screen. 'Check it out. We're playing trivia.'

'Better hope the questions are at a high-school level.'

Danny raises his eyebrows. 'I'll teach her everything she needs to know.'

'Get fucked,' says Cal. 'You're cooked.'

'Why? Ms Jacobs taught me and she was way older.'

Cal groans. 'Still clinging to that Ms Jacobs story?'

'I'm only using her as a standard unit of measurement. Don't tell me you've forgotten how hot she was.'

As much as he wants to, Cal can't argue with Danny. Ms Jacobs had been their geography teacher at school and, well, yeah, she was hot. No question. They ran into her at the pub a couple of years back–maybe three months after graduating–and spent the night drinking together. Cal and Liam watched on as she and Danny flirted with each other, touching arms and legs and laughing at every dumb joke. They went to get drinks for the table and were gone for ages; too long, Liam argued, for them to be having sex, but Danny eventually returned and told them that he'd fucked Ms Jacobs in the toilet. He didn't seem surprised either; more like, it was only a matter of time. He sounded like a man who had come into himself, rather than his teacher. He's sounded that way ever since.

'She must be at least forty now,' says Cal. He'd been as excited as anyone about Danny and Ms Jacobs, but now it weirded him out.

'Age shall not weary her, nor the years condemn. We will remember her.'

'The ANZACs? Really?'

Danny bows his head. 'A minute's silence, please.'

Cal sighs. He knows Danny won't relent unless he joins him, so he bows his head and retreats to his memories of that night at the pub, of the conversation he had with Liam around a heavy wooden table in the red-brick courtyard. It was a conversation that began and ended with

Liam in tears. He told Cal that he needed to get out of there; out of the pub, out of Sydney, out of fucking Australia, if that's what it took.

He told Cal that he needed an escape route.

Room to breathe.

He asked Cal if he understood and Cal didn't know what to say. Did he understand? No. Did he want to understand? Again, not really. What he wanted was to have one night out without it turning to shit because Liam couldn't pull himself together, but how do you say that to a friend?

Cal now knows that the answer is this: you don't.

But with five schooners in his bloodstream and summer in the air, Cal told Liam the truth. He'd do anything to put things right, to live in a world where Ms Jacobs was nothing to them but a geography teacher and Liam felt understood, or less alone, but Cal knows the ten-hour difference between Sydney and London is the closest he'll ever come to going back in time. And ten hours just isn't enough.

Sixty seconds tick by. 'Lest we forget,' says Danny, pouring a drop of beer on the seat between them. 'For those who couldn't come. And those who made me.'

'Gross,' says Cal, pretending to reach for a sick bag. 'Happy now?'

'Very.'

The two boys return to their screens; Danny to his conversation with 13F, Cal to his bullshit movie, which insists that hope and light can be found in even the darkest of times.

Hope.

Ha.

Cal doesn't deserve hope. He couldn't give it to Liam, so how can he claim it for himself? The priest had spoken about hope at Liam's funeral. Cal and Danny drove hours from Sydney to be there, in the town where Liam, a border, had grown up, and they crossed the baked earth of the church yard in solemn silence. They wore Hawaiian shirts–Liam's favourite–and shook their heads at how ridiculous, how forced it all felt.

'For I know the plans I have for you, declares the Lord. Plans for welfare and not for evil, to give you a future and a hope.

Words from a god that Liam had never believed in, from a god that had never believed in Liam. What future? What hope? The priest told those in the packed-out church that they mustn't lose hope; in the Lord, in each other. He gave them permission to feel anger towards Liam for doing something so stupid, but sitting in that back-breaking pew, Cal felt nothing but guilt.

For knowing something was wrong, but not knowing how to help.

For knowing he should say something, but lacking the vocabulary.

For allowing Liam's heart to break long before his neck.

These thoughts, those memories, they batter Cal's defences constantly, determined to find a way through like the predatory sunlight behind the plane's window shade. Cal opens it and golden light floods the cabin, forcing Danny to cover his eyes.

'What the fuck? Cal, I'm working here.'

'You don't actually think you're going to get lucky, right? The mile-high club is a myth. It doesn't happen in real life.'

'This has always been your problem,' says Danny. 'Have some confidence for once. Some faith.'

Cal shakes his head, his gut trying to calm the inner-turbulence that's become so familiar. 'How can you have faith?' he says. 'Liam's dead, Danny. He killed himself. We're his best mates and we're going on a fucking holiday.'

'It's what he would've wanted.'

'I feel like we need to talk about it or something.'

'What's to talk about? It's done. We can't change that. Maybe it was his time.'

'Don't you feel guilty? Like, I don't know, like we're somehow responsible? Like we could've done more?'

'I'm okay,' says Danny, pulling his headphones out of his pocket and stuffing a bud in each ear. 'Seriously. I'm okay.'

'Yeah? Man, I don't know if I am.'

Danny shrugs and points to his ears, mouths that he can't hear what Cal is saying. With the conversation seemingly over, Cal tries to climb over Danny and into the aisle, but Danny punches him on the way through and gives him a dead leg. Swearing, Cal limps to the toilet at the back of the plane.

It's occupied.

He stands awkwardly by the door, stretching his back, his legs, moving aside for the steady stream of flight attendants. One of them offers him an extra packet of crackers and as he's crunching through it he sees 13F, the blonde girl, making her way up the aisle towards him. He freezes.

'Hey,' she says. 'Your friend. Is he okay?'

Cal figures she's referring to Danny's shit chat. 'He's not a bad guy,' he says, hands fumbling at the cracker packet. 'I think he thinks you're older than you are and, you know, you're obviously very pretty, and yeah, I'm sorry about him. Our friend died and it's been a hard couple of weeks. I think he's lonely, to be honest. Yeah. Lonely. Which I guess is why he's been messaging you.'

'What? What messages?'

'On the screen? The in-flight messages?'

'I've got no idea what you're on about. If he's talking to someone, it's not me.'

'Then why are you asking if he's okay?'

She jerks her head back down the aisle. 'Because he's sitting there crying for some reason. And I saw that you guys were together earlier. In the food court. I thought you'd want to know.'

Cal nods, points to the cracker packet, to his full mouth.

'I'm Bel, by the way.'

He forces himself to swallow. Coughs. Splutters. Dies inside. 'I'm Cal.'

'And I'm twenty,' she says, smiling. 'In case you were wondering.'

Cal's cheeks glow bright red in the light of the newly vacated bathroom. He and Bel flatten themselves against the wall to allow the man to pass and Cal, flustered, gestures at Bel to go first. She thanks him, but doesn't invite him in, proving beyond all doubt that the mile-high club is a myth. Once she's finished, she holds the door open and tells him that she's sitting in 12F. Again, in case he was wondering.

Wanting to give Danny a chance to collect himself, Cal kills time in the bathroom before taking the scenic route back to his seat. He walks past row twelve, grinning at Bel, and checks out Danny's mystery pen pal in row thirteen before looping around to his own seat. He parries Danny's punches as he clambers across to the window.

'Alright?' says Cal, fastening his seatbelt.

Danny nods; red eyes, big grin. 'Never better. This chick is really cool. Way more mature than you'd think.'

'Oh yeah?' Cal isn't surprised, given the man sat in 13F looks to be approaching fifty. He considers telling Danny, but they've a long flight ahead of them and it feels like forever since he's had something to smile about.

Instead, Cal lifts his window shade and peers through the portal. The sky has split in two: light behind them, darkness ahead. There are no stars, no smoking engines. Nothing. Not even another plane, though Cal knows there must be hundreds out there, all flying north for the winter. They'll be carrying people like him and Danny. People armed with backpacks, Birkenstocks and battle-hardened livers.

Or maybe they won't be.

Maybe, instead of people like him and Danny, the planes will be carrying people like Liam. Cal has seen the numbers, knows them off by heart. He does the math and decides it would take around 134 planes, depending on the seating configuration, to carry everyone who has tried this year. Seven for those who have succeeded, five reserved for the men alone.

That's where Liam will be, Cal figures.

Seatbelt fastened, a beer in his hand, the plane hurtling to the ground as the men around him–the dads, the brothers, the sons–all tell each other the same thing: I'm okay.

How do you feel now?
S.S. Turner

The man known across the Australian advertising world as the 'How do you feel' guy shifted on his feet with the nervousness of a younger, less confident man. His jacket was at least an inch too tight around the middle, so he'd have to restrain himself in the event something funny happened. It wouldn't be a good look to laugh freely and inadvertently shoot a suit button at one of the four people gazing up at him from around the boardroom table. He guesstimated he had enough laughter brewing inside to turn any button into an explosive bullet—it was a comforting thought. The two women and two men were staring at him, willing him to get on with it, whatever it was. They were all dressed in the same brand new shiny business attire, all thirty-something years old, with the same modern day listlessness in their eyes. But it was their lucky day—he was there to lighten their moods.

'Please introduce yourself, Mr?' asked a woman wearing sharp-rimmed spectacles which could have cut through aged cheddar.

'Yes, of course,' he responded with a broad smile and growing confidence. 'I'll let this video make my introduction for me.'

The woman exhaled a huff of despair. Surely he understood she wanted words which saved time, because time was money in the fast-paced advertising world in which he was standing. But he didn't understand. He pressed play on the video. Like a well-trained orchestra conductor, he stood back from the screen so everyone could view the main players. He didn't want anyone to miss out.

A green cricket ground emerged on the fuzzy screen, followed by two cricket players dressed in white who were walking with purpose. One carried a cricket bat, and the other rubbed a cricket ball into the red-stained patch at the top of his trousers. Their messy haircuts and blatantly hairy chests advertised a simpler time when men didn't care about little things like grooming.

A song started playing with the scratchy acoustics of an earlier era: 'How do you feel? When you walk on the field knowing you're the last to play?'. The bowler sprinted in to bowl.

The man gazed around the room. Unsurprisingly, the audience was engrossed by the video. He'd been right to play it. The song continued: 'How do you feel? When you face a new ball and a win is just five runs away?' The bowler launched the ball directly at the wicket with the finesse he was famous for. The man watched on full of pride for the bowler, for the video, for what it represented.

'Excuse me?' called out a man with slicked back hair wearing a pin-striped suit. 'Can we skip the rest, please? You know how it is. Limited time and all that.'

The man thought he must have misheard him. 'But we're just getting to the best bit,' he stated. 'The umpire is about to reject his appeal.'

'I know how he feels,' said the slick-haired man. 'Can you please just introduce yourself? Who are you?'

The man regathered himself. He kicked the esky full of icy cold Tooheys beer cans back under the table. He tried to forget how fulfilling it would have been to have thrown a few coldies across the table at the end of the video as he'd planned to do. It never failed to rouse the rabble. He reminded himself he was the 'How do you feel' guy regardless.

'Monty Summers at your service,' he stated with a bow.

'Can you tell us about yourself, please?' asked a yellow-suited woman who'd started typing notes on her computer.

'It's Summers, like the cricket season,' he stated. 'Do you want me to spell that for you?'

'No, thanks,' she responded, 'I'd just like to understand who you are.'

'Well, it's all so simple. I'm the guy who wrote those commercials,' he said pointing at the frozen screen behind him.

'And what was it a commercial for?' asked the typist with faster typing skills than were required considering Monty Summers' pace of speech.

'What? You don't know it?' replied a flabbergasted Monty Summers. 'Shall I play it through to the end? I'm sure you'll recognize the chorus. That was cricket legend Denis Lilee bowling, and I wrote the words to the song.'

'No thanks, Mr Lilee,' said the manic typist.

'No, I'm Mr Summers. Lilee was the bowler in the video. Are you taking the piss?' he asked with genuine concern for all their wellbeing.

'We're just trying to establish why we should consider working with you as an advert writer, Mr Summers,' responded a rotund man with a disengaged air who'd been quiet up until that point. 'We'd appreciate you humoring us.'

Monty Summers laughed out loud and lost control of his not insignificant belly for a split second. Humor them he bloody well would. Then remembered the fragile state of his buttons and peered down. Luckily, his suit jacket remained buttoned up, but two of the buttons were sitting at sharp angles which suggested they'd been tested and found wanting.

'OK, I'll humor you,' Monty Summers replied. 'It's an advert for Tooheys, and it's arguably the most culturally significant advert in Australian history. Some would say it represents the very heart of Australian culture. Surely you all know this already?'

'Tooheys, the beer?' asked the typist.

'Yes, the bloody beer,' replied an angry Monty Summers. Who didn't know what Tooheys was? He was starting to suspect these people were from another planet, and one he didn't want to visit.

'Here's a question for you, Mr Summers,' said the sharp-spectacled woman. 'When was that advert made?'

'When Australia ruled the cricketing world: 1979,' stated a proud Monty Summers. 'Lilee was a legend. The Tooheys' adverts cemented his position in Australian folklore.'

'So, that's forty-three years ago,' continued the sharp-spectacled woman. 'You must have been a young man when you wrote it?'

'Yes, I was only twenty-five at the time,' responded Monty Summers as he stood a little taller. He wondered if the women in the audience had noticed his arms still had muscle tone. He flexed for their benefit. As he did, his entire upper body erupted into more simultaneous rigidity than he was prepared for–like a bodybuilder in the winning photo shot. However, Monty Summers wasn't a bodybuilder. He was a sixty-eight-year-old man with uncontrollable man boobs. He was also in need of work. He tried to compensate for the abrupt upper body gyrations by relaxing back into a more natural posture. But his efforts were redundant. He breathed out his frustration, and the sharp-angled buttons decided that was their moment to launch. They both shot out into the air in front of Monty Summers, before crash-landing onto the boardroom table with louder clinks than he would have guessed possible. Sweat dripped off Monty Summers' forehead as he wished himself anywhere but there. The two men and two women stared at the two stationery buttons as though they were idiotic gate-crashers at an exclusive party for intellectuals. Monty Summers also stared at the rogue buttons which had gone and stolen his show.

'How do you think Australia has changed since you wrote that advert?' interjected the typist with growing urgency.

'Well, for starters, the Australian cricket team doesn't have the same number of dead-set legends in it these days,' replied Monty Summers with a reflective nod.

'I meant in terms of the big picture,' added the typist who'd stopped typing because Monty Summers wasn't making type-worthy comments, and probably never had. 'You know, things like national identity, the wellbeing of indigenous Australians, the relationship between the sexes, toxic masculinity, and what's considered appropriate.'

'Oh,' responded Monty Summers with less enthusiasm. 'Well, I suppose there have been a few changes. I certainly watch what I say around the ladies more than I used to.'

The rotund disengaged man suddenly stood up, suddenly engaged. He marched up to the front of the room where Monty Summers had previously been the only one standing. He was at least six foot six. Monty Summers wished he'd sit back down and stop making him feel so bloody short. But the tall rotund man didn't sit back down. Instead, he pushed a whiteboard in front of the projector screen as though he was the teacher and everyone else were students. Monty Summers didn't know whether to remain standing like a teacher's aide, or to sit down like a pesky student. He hovered without purpose.

'Mr Summers,' said the tall rotund man as he stood even taller, pulled out a whiteboard pen from inside his jacket, and drew two perfect circles on the whiteboard, 'these two circles represent Australia in 1979 and in 2022. We're interested by how much the heart of Australian culture, as you referred to, has changed in those forty-three years.'

Monty Summers sensed the conversation was heading in a direction he didn't want it to. Sitting down was fast becoming his best option, his only option, so he sat down in the nearest spare seat. He wished himself invisible.

'Let's start with 1979 Australian culture,' continued the tall rotund man with a tall rotund voice. 'What are the best words we can use to describe it, gang?'

'Free!' said Monty Summers without meaning to voice the first opinion.

'Boozy,' added the yellow-suited woman.

'Hear! Hear!' exclaimed Monty Summers.

'Chauvinistic,' stated the typist as she typed out the word for extra emphasis.

'Wild,' said the slick-haired man.

'And I'm going to add sports obsessed,' contributed the tall rotund man.

'They were the days, eh?' added Monty Summers with a grin.

The yellow-suited woman let out a harsh high-pitched chuckle which made it clear to all present that she was amused by Monty Summers in the most condescending of ways. The tall rotund man ignored the raucousness as he was still writing words in the left-hand circle. Monty Summers noticed he was writing in lower case letters when upper case seemed more appropriate.

'And now, gang, what are the best words to describe 2022 Australian culture?' asked the tall rotund man with growing gravity.

A heavy silence weighed upon the room as everyone racked their brains for just the right words.

'I'm sticking with free,' stated Monty Summers with less confidence than the first time he'd said it.

However, the tall rotund man appeared to have misheard him as he didn't write the word on the board.

'In transition?' asked the yellow-suited woman.

The tall rotund man nodded and wrote the words on the board.

'Conciliatory,' added the slick-haired man, and the tall rotund man wrote it down.

'Healing,' stated the typist as she typed the word slowly.

The tall rotund man thought for a moment, shrugged his shoulders, and added it to the whiteboard.

'I'm going even further than that, guys,' said the tall rotund man as he added the word 'lost' to the right hand circle.

Without planning to, Monty Summers jumped up out of his seat and stood to attention. The slick-haired man grabbed his phone from the table revealing to all that he thought Monty Summers may attempt to steal it from under his very nose. But Monty Summers had bigger fish to fry.

'Who are you people?' he asked. 'Are you really telling me you think Australia is lost.

I take offence at that and I won't stand for it anymore.'

'What's really upsetting to you, Mr Summers?' asked the tall rotund man as he stepped toward Monty Summers who in turn took a step away from him to avoid being hit, or even worse, being made to look small.

'Well, it's not right, is it?' half-stated, half-asked Monty Summers. 'This is the best country in the world, everyone knows that.'

The tall rotund man walked back to the whiteboard, and pointed at the 1979 Australia circle.

'Mr Summers, I can see why you are so enthusiastic about 1979 Australia,' he stated as he removed the lid from the pen in preparation for some more unwelcome writing action. 'And I've got two more words to add to that circle.'

He then wrote the words 'Monty Summers' in the 1979 Australia circle, before he crossed out the entire circle as though it had all been a terrible mistake in the first place.

Monty Summers marched up to the whiteboard and ripped the pen out of the tall rotund man's hand. The larger man didn't attempt to stop him. He even appeared ready to hand the pen over. And then, Monty Summers wrote two words in capital letters in the 2022 Australia circle: 'UNGRATEFUL BASTARDS'.

The room fell silent as everyone digested Monty Summers' awful addition to the circle. The manic typist decided his words weren't worthy of being typed, so she typed the words 'mentally unstable' instead. The tall rotund man stepped forward with purpose.

'Here's where you're confused, Mr Summers,' the tall rotund man stated with more kindness than everyone had expected. 'The Australia you want to hold onto was an earlier version of an old country masquerading as a new country. You were no doubt a great contributor to the cultural heart of that version of this country.'

Monty Summers shuffled away from the whiteboard, and sat back down. These people had a way of making him feel stupid, and he was tired of feeling stupid.

'But the country is lost, is in transition, is conciliatory, and is healing these days. And that's exactly as it should be,' the tall man continued. 'The party is over because we were only gate-crashers in the first place. And out of this cultural chasm will emerge something far more significant and meaningful than any beer song at the cricket. That won't stop people from singing your song with you, and for you, Mr Summers. But it will mean there will also be songs to be sung about Indigenous Australians, caring for our environment, and the diverse range of cultures living here in 2022. These issues are surely bigger than getting drunk and throwing a ball around. How do you feel about that, Mr Summers?'

Monty Summers eyed up the esky full of cold Tooheys cans sitting underneath the table as he carefully considered his response. 'The truth is this modern version of Australia requires a cold beer to make any sense out it. I just feel like a Tooheys or two,' he half-whispered.

Monty Summers retired hurt that very afternoon.

Intangible Binds
Tanya Park

'Htt, two, three, four.'

At the loud command accompanied by a sharp shove in the ribs, Florence sighed then eased her tired old limbs from the tangle of bedclothes. It felt as though she had only just closed her eyes and didn't appreciate being woken. Wriggling her feet to the floor, she reached across to the rocker for her candlewick dressing gown and shoved her arms into the sleeves.

'Stand at atten - tion!'

At the barked order from her right she straightened her back, snapped her heels together, dropped her left hand stiff and straight by her side, ignoring the gown as it began to slither from her shoulder. Her right arm bent at the elbow; fingers stretched straight as they touched the hairline of her snow-white hair in a perfect salute.

Moving only her eyes while waiting for the order to be released from the stiff stance, Florence glanced at the clock. Two thirty-five in the morning. Only two hours rest. Not nearly enough. She dared a grimace, both annoyed and amused at this ritual, which occurred more and more often. This was the third time this week.

Still at attention, the coldness of the night air invaded the thin cotton of her nightie and settled against her skin as the robe slid further down one side. The other side was still held in place by her raised arm. Knowing he wouldn't notice in the gloom of the darkness, she inched her left arm away from her body a fraction, allowed the dressing gown freedom to fall until it hung from her right shoulder.

'Stand at…ease!'

At the barked words, Florence dropped her right hand down to her side, leaving enough space for the gown to slither in silence to the ground. He wouldn't notice, wouldn't see. As she moved her feet apart to balance her weight in the easy stance, she gave the gown a slight kick with her foot so it wasn't in the way for what was to come next.

To gain any peace and a few more hours' sleep, she'd learnt it was best to comply with his orders until his fragile mind caught up with the present and he dropped back into a restless doze.

'Set, march!' he yelled in his stern sergeant's voice. 'Htt, two, three, four. Htt, two three, four.'

As the rhythmic tone of his voice repeated the phrase over and over, Florence moved her eighty-year-old legs in time, marched across the floor with stiff arms swinging - forwards, backwards, left, right, left, right; head up, eyes ahead - forwards, backwards, left, right.

Once through the open door she marked time in the passage so he could still hear the hypnotic rhythm of feet hitting the frigid polished floorboards. Left, right, left, right, thump, thump, thump, thump. She smiled as she dared a peek around the painted doorframe to see if he still sat up rigid in the bed or if he was sinking back down onto the pillows.

It had taken several nights of marching around and around the room until her legs ached and her arms turned to jellified rubber before she discovered this trick. If he heard the slap, slap, slap of feet hitting the floorboards in time with his calls, he was happy his regiment was marching. Soon his voice would tire, his eyes close and he would sink back to the mattress. She figured he always dreamed in the past when asleep because during the hours he was awake, it was rare for him to recognise the present.

Still marching in time, Florence focussed on her thoughts to while away the time. It had been a gradual process at first. Just a few lapses when he would forget what he had been talking about. Then the blanks became more regular, lasting longer each time. It hadn't been so noticeable at first because those around him filled in the gaps but when it was just the two of them, she soon realised his present memory was fading away and there wasn't a darn thing she could do to help him.

Then confusion set in, especially when any of their children visited. He knew they were his children but would go through the entire list of names, male and female, of all six offspring, never knowing which one he was speaking to. He even included the name of the son who died in infancy fifty-five years earlier.

The next stage was forgetting how to complete simple automatic tasks. No longer could he draw the intricate cartoons he was so famous for. Put a pencil in his fingers now and all he could do was stare at it as though it was an alien object. He couldn't even draw a circle; didn't know what a circle was.

As she peeked around the door to see if his body had flagged as much as hers, Florence noticed his dishevelled hair. The few remaining strands stood on end. The sight brought her thoughts to another aspect of his memory loss. Basic hygiene skills had gone by the board. This time last year she could layer the bristles of his toothbrush with paste and he knew how to brush his teeth. Now…well now it was a fight to get the brush into his mouth for her to scrub away. He fought back as though he was being brutally attacked.

For something to keep her mind occupied, her eyes scouted around the hallway lit by a night-light. She focussed on a row of photographs hanging the length of one wall: eleven grandchildren in order of birth. Now, it was difficult when a grandchild arrived to visit and even more awkward when two or more arrived at the same time. Her husband stared blankly at them, some niggling stab seeming to tell him he knew this person but not having a clue as to who stood in front of him or what to call them. Frustrated at not being able to recall, he was often terse, causing tension, the recipient of his angry words wondering why on earth they bothered calling since he couldn't remember, or talk to them, then vowing to never come again. But they always did.

With the biting cold becoming too much, Florence glanced around the doorframe again. 'Thank goodness,' she whispered into the silence as she noted her much-loved husband had fallen sideways. His voice still counted to four but the tone had lost its demanding edge and the words were now slurred. Still she lifted her feet in time, knowing that to cease before he stopped counting would re-waken him. He would become alert and the entire process would begin again. Better to keep going a few minutes more than to start over.

Her body trembled from the cold as her knees bent and lifted, one after the other but not as high, not as determined. Shivering, she waited, watched, listened until she was certain he was no longer aware. Her feet stilled while her breath held.

Silence.

Her footsteps were whisper quiet, shushing against the carpet as she crossed the room. She stood beside his relaxed, sleeping body for a moment before she rolled him into a more comfortable position, the action difficult since she was so tiny, not even reaching the five-foot mark when fully stretched. It took a few seconds of gentle tugging to unravel the crumpled covers, pull them to his shoulders and tuck the ends in to keep him warm. Love poured from her eyes as she patted him on the shoulder then stooped to plant a gentle kiss on his brow. 'I love you, dear,' she whispered, 'but this is becoming too hard.'

As she padded around to the other side of the bed, her bones ached but as always, she ignored her own discomfort. There was no point in saying anything. He didn't understand and who else was there to care for him? The children were scattered around the world with jobs, lives and families of their own. Two daughters lived a few hours away while only their eldest son, David, lived in the property behind. But he was married and worked long hours. He did what he could with the house and garden maintenance plus he, or his wife, Pat, called every morning and evening to check on them.

Taking her time, Florence eased back into bed and lay back on the pillow while she enveloped her frozen flesh in the covers, seeking what little warmth they still afforded. She knew from experience it would take a while before the bed warmed again, for her shivers to cease, for her to gain the sleep she so desperately needed.

Her eyes skittered across the ceiling, not really focussing on anything even though she could make out vague shapes in the light from the half moon and the soft glow from the passage. In her mind, she tossed around the same old argument. When could she no longer manage to care for him? Was it time yet? Could she let him go? Their life hadn't been easy with money often short, but he had always provided for his family, even in those long years he fought in wars overseas.

A career soldier, he had run away from home and lied about his age, adding two years to his fourteen to enable him to fight in the second Boer war. She smiled into the darkness. That was before they were sweethearts, even though they knew each other. Her smile changed to a grimace as her thoughts swung to the first world war where a bullet shattered his right knee and left him with a permanent limp. The injury had killed his career as a gymnastics instructor and prevented him from competing at Olympic level in men's gymnastics, for which he had trained long hours. It was after he returned home to recuperate they had dated, then wed.

Hearing all about the better life in Australia, they emigrated to begin a new life. He earned enough money as a skilled carpenter making superior quality furniture, to keep his ever-increasing family housed, clothed and fed, until the Second World War began. Unable to resist the lure of the Army life he loved so much, he again lied about his age, this time deducting a couple of years to be eligible to enlist once again. Unable to fight on the front because of his gammy leg, he spent the years as a training sergeant at Blackboy Hill, instructing recruits, teaching necessary skills, discipline and marching, marching, marching.

Florence turned over to ease the ache in her hip; the ache she knew was permanent. Old Mr Arthritis had paid a visit and refused to leave. She told no one, not even her doctor, for they would insist her darling husband go into a nursing home. To her it meant they would have to live apart and she knew, deep in her heart - he wouldn't survive if they were separated. She loved him dearly but sometimes, when he was at his most difficult, it was hard to remember why, especially now with her broken nights marching, as he relived his soldiering years.

She smiled in the dim light at the thought of marching. With his bouts living in the past, she wasn't sure which war he was fighting in, but she suspected his memory was now centred in Africa, fighting the Boers.

As the lights from a passing car danced across the wall opposite the window, Florence followed the sinuous line with her eyes until it disappeared but even then, she listened to the swish of tyres and the humming engine until it faded into the distance. What else was there to do in the long minutes and hours while waiting for sleep to claim you once again? Every sound, every movement was a welcome relief from the tedium of lying in bed, wide-awake, just thinking, thinking, thinking.

Her thoughts drifted to the past twenty years. Twenty years of his body succumbing to the effects of the long months spent huddled in flooded, filthy trenches, always drenched to the bone or stifling in the heat. Twenty years of the shrapnel remnants caused an ever-increasing discomfort and pain. Twenty years of rheumatoid arthritis setting in and worsening every week, every month, every year. At first it wasn't so bad. With a clear mind and reasoning, he could understand and manage his increasing disability. It might have taken time for him to complete his ablutions, to dress and move from room to room but he didn't require her twenty-four-hour assistance.

But now, it wasn't only a fragile mind she had to cope with but also a fragile body: fragile in every part, except for his heart. The doctor continually marvelled at how strong his heart was for a man approaching ninety. When things were really bad, Florence often decried the strength of his heart. Sometimes she prayed his heart would give out, so he didn't have to suffer any longer. But then, it wasn't him suffering the most. He rarely remembered, rarely knew. Guilt stabbed for daring to have those wishes because, in reality, it was a desire for her to be released from the hourly grind of nursing care of someone who was almost in a constant vegetative state.

It felt as though she had only just gone back to sleep when she was woken again.

'Flo, toilet, now!'

Barely awake, Florence shot from the bed, suppressed the groan of pain as her legs hit the ground.

'Flo, hurry.'

Despite the anxiety in his words, Florence grinned and her heart swelled in her tiny chest. For him to call her Flo, and ask to go to the toilet, his mind was in the present. She rushed around to the other side of the bed with a heart-stopping smile spread across her face, grasped the handles of the wheelchair commode and set it in place.

'Good morning, Dear,' she said as she ensured the brakes were locked. She dragged back the covers, grabbed the waistband of his pyjama pants and yanked them from his legs in one swift movement.

'Where have you been, Flo?'

A tear surged, then crept from the corner of her eye. How to answer, she thought as her hands moved to his armpits where she slid her arms under and around his back? 'I'm always nearby, Dear.' One almighty heave had him sitting upright but she gasped out aloud when a sharp twinge in her back sliced through her as though being stabbed and sawn with a serrated knife. Ignoring the pain, she slid his legs over the side of the bed, placed his hands on her shoulders.

Tension tightened every muscle in her body as she supported his ninety-kilo weight with her fifty while she swung his body around from the bed to the seat. Her solitary tear turned to a flood as the continuous piercing pain in her back sawed through her flesh. What took less than a minute, seemed like an hour with the unrelenting ripping agony.

The daily morning ritual had begun but deep down, Florence knew.

Today she wasn't going to be able to cope. He needed a sponge bath, to be dressed and fed. It usually took a tremendous amount of time and patience to coax his unco-operative body, to work fighting limbs into clothes and pull them into place before buttoning or zipping apertures closed. Feeding him was no different from feeding a recalcitrant baby, one spoon at a time, wiping at the dribbles and encouraging him to chew and swallow.

After easing him back onto the side of the bed, Florence finally released her grip on his body and sagged against the edge of the bed, her arms stretched out to support her weight as she leant over with her fingers clutching tight at the edge of the mattress.

She couldn't breathe.

The slightest movement caused a searing sharp pain to radiate from her lower spine outwards, outwards, outwards. She needed help. Settling him back against the pillows with her held breath fighting against her pain, she drew the covers over his nudity to keep him warm.

'I'll be right back, dear.'

He gave her a strange look. 'Who are you?' he asked in a terse voice, his brief foray into reality now passed.

Fighting back tears she never allowed anyone to see, she straightened, bit her lower lip at the agony. Forced to take it very slow, she shuffled across the room, down the passage and into the kitchen, not once daring to pause for if she stopped, she wouldn't be able to get going again. Reaching the telephone, her held breath gushed out as she gingerly slumped against the wall for support and dialled for David.

'David, it's Mum, please, I need you now.' Not even having the strength to hang up, her breath stuttered as she eased into the ornate chair by the telephone, where she remained without moving until her son arrived through the back corner gate from the house behind.

It took two eternal hours before Florence received relief from her agony. Lying in a hospital bed, the painkillers had finally kicked in. She couldn't move, didn't dare move, the shredded muscles and tendons she'd torn in her back forcing her to have the rest she had refused for the past twenty years. But she knew it was only a reprieve. Once her injuries healed, she would be back to the old tedium until such time her darling husband's still strong heart ran out of beats. Even though her eyes kept sliding closed, she didn't sleep, worry refusing to allow her mind to relax.

'Mum?'

Her eyes flew open. 'David? How's Dad? Who's caring for him?'

'Relax, Mum. The doctor found an emergency bed in Pat's nursing home. Dad's there now and Pat is on duty. She's caring for him. The important thing now is for you to take care of yourself.'

'I can't not worry about him.' A single tear slid from the corner of her eye. David leant over and gently swept it away with the crook of his finger. The warmth and tenderness of his touch was almost her undoing. She fought back the desperate urge to cry and then cry some more but she had never let her children see her being weak–and couldn't start now. His large hand settled over her clenched fists, the tender warmth easing her tension and stilling her agitation.

'Let me do the worrying while you concentrate on getting better. Dad is in excellent hands. As soon as you are out of here, you can spend as much time as you want sitting with him in the nursing home. Now sleep.'

It took two weeks of recuperation and intensive physiotherapy before Florence was allowed home. The emptiness and sense of loss slammed into her like a tornado the moment she entered the back door. Overwhelmed, she stood on the threshold for a moment. The silence was unnerving. Someone had been in to clean. Her twitching nose sensed the presence of the recent use of unfamiliar cleaning chemicals but underneath the aroma she was still able to detect familiar scents.

Traces of her husband's aftershave wafted and brought out a smile. He had always been particular about being clean-shaven, having unmussed hair, dressed in long-sleeved white shirt and immaculately pressed trousers. Never would he tolerate being slovenly dressed.

Even though her son was being solicitous in ensuring she was settled in, Florence prayed he would hurry up and leave. Much as she loved him and knew he was concerned about her, all she wanted was to be alone: alone in her home, alone to think, alone to breathe in the essence of her husband. She hadn't seen him for two whole weeks.

Every day was a struggle. Her age meant torn tendons took a long time to heal. But, by taking her time to carry out each menial task, she managed everyday living on her own, telling her family only the positives and failing to mention the mishaps like when she stumbled and fell. The resultant large blue bruise was sore but hidden under clothes so they would never know. Nor would they know how she dropped the tray containing her freshly prepared lunch because it had been a tad too heavy, or the effort it had taken for her to drop to her knees to clean up the mess. Rising upright again had taken its toll. Crawling to a chair to use as support had been the only way she had been able to stand. The pain had been excruciating.

She decried the need for the physiotherapist who came every few days to massage and carefully watch as Florence undertook exercises. At the same time, the exercises were working. She also hated how two of her daughters arrived on different days of the week, bringing food and basic necessities then dusting, cleaning or whatever household chore needed doing.

She enjoyed the visits, chats and the rides to the nursing home but at the same time, wished they would leave her in peace. Nobody could do things the way she wanted, the way she was used to. Ornaments weren't put back in the exact same place and her laundry wasn't folded the way she preferred. They dusted but she liked to have her furniture, the furniture her husband had made for her over the years, polished until it gleamed.

Even though she struggled, every day her health improved a tiny bit more. She could feel her back mending; could feel the renewed ease in how she moved. Each day she was able to do a little extra. The relief was intense at not having to constantly nurse her ailing husband but at the same time there was tremendous guilt at not being by his side to care for him. Guilt far outweighed relief.

Each day she visited him in the afternoon, at first by taxi if it wasn't one of the days her children were able to drive her. Then she tested her driving ability and even though it still hurt to ease her body into the little blue Mini-Minor, she began to drive herself to the shops and nursing home every day, relishing the freedom.

Her greatest joy was singing to her husband; singing the old songs, even the dirty army ditties that caused her cheeks to warm and redden in embarrassment. For it was one thing his mind hadn't forgotten. He remembered all the words and would sing along with her, even smiling and laughing at the naughty phrases. But even though he joined in, she knew.

In the deepest recesses of her soul she knew he was fading–giving up the will to live. And she knew it was because somewhere in the equally deep recesses of his befuddled mind, he knew she wasn't there caring for him.

Often, she pulled a few old photographs from her bag and held them in front of his eyes. Depending on his state of mind, he would stare at them. Mostly, he reacted to the photos of either him or her as youngsters. She lived for the odd occasions when he pointed to a photo of her as a young woman and said, 'that's my sweetheart - my Florence. I'm going to marry her one day.'

It was almost six weeks after her accident when Florence was preparing her evening meal at the kitchen sink while she stared out the window over-looking the only pathway to the back of the house. Her thoughts lingered on her husband. They'd had a wonderful afternoon, with him in a happy frame of mind. As she peeled the skin from a carrot, she was most surprised to hear a loud knock on the back door.

'Who's there?' she called.

Silence.

Unnerved, she settled the vegetable peeler and carrot on the bench as she leant over the sink and peered through the window to search both ways up and down the pathway no-one had walked along. There was no sign of anyone.

A second rap at the door stilled her. Neither David nor Pat would be home from work yet, besides, they had their own key and always called out as they entered. She crept across the kitchen, stood in the doorway of the laundry and stared at the back door, mystified.

A third, much louder rap sounded. Creeping to the small side window next to the solid wooden door, she twitched the edge of the curtain just far enough so she could peek out. There was no-one, no shadow, no movement.

While she watched, a fourth knock came, louder still. Positive no-one was there because she could see clearly with her own eyes, she was completely baffled and a more than little afraid.

A sudden shiver passed through her as something warm kissed against her skin. A solitary tear ran down her cheek. A weird sensation: a warm aura, settled over and around her like a soft mantle. She smiled.

The telephone rang. She hurried to answer it. 'Hello.'

'Mrs Williamson?'

'Yes.' Her breath caught and held.

'I'm sorry to tell you but your husband has just passed away.'

'I know,' she said. 'He just called in to say goodbye.'

All Weather
A'Mhara Mckey

It's a blue-sky day in August and my knees protest as I pluck tiny green caterpillars off my roses. The chickens love 'em, but the cheap foam kneeling pad I got from Bunnings just isn't cutting it. Should've gone with the Garden Kneeler with its extra thick padding and handles.

There was a late frost last night and my breath puffs out in clouds. Not the best day to be in the garden, but Tuesday's gardening day. Rain, hail or shine.

'It'll kill the geraniums,' my neighbour warns me as she walks past with the squashed-nosed French bulldog she calls Josephine. 'Should've put them inside last night.'

I give her that tight smile I reserve for people who take pleasure in pointing out the obvious.

'Oh well,' she goes on, 'lessons learned and all that.'

She moves on and I glare at her extra-wide behind as she walks towards Cranston Road. Josephine the bulldog looks back at me, tongue lolling. She's breathing like a pack-a-day smoker.

Brachycephalic Airway Syndrome. My old boxer Bruno had that and died during the surgery to fix it. Still haven't paid the vet bill.

A trail of mutilated leaves leads me to three caterpillars who hit the water at the bottom of the bucket with hardly a splash.

Raised voices catch my attention. I struggle to my feet with a groan. The ergonomic handles of the Garden Kneeler suddenly seem value for money. From my front gate, I can just see the vacant lot on the corner. A group of people are clustered around something in the too-long grass. Hands are waving, someone's on their phone. If I walk down, I could find out what was happening, but you know what they say about curiosity and the cat.

Besides, it's nine o'clock. Teatime.

But first, I need the loo. There was a time when everything down there worked regular. Now it was a gamble whether I'd make it in time or not.

I'm washing my tea mug when someone knocks. The only visitors I get are Jehovah's Witnesses and people collecting for charity. The god botherers are the lesser evil. At least they don't want my credit card details.

I open the door to find a young police officer on my doorstep. My heart flutters uncomfortably when she takes off her hat, just like with the one who came to tell me my brother was dead.

'What's this then?'

Josephine lies on the mat outside my back door, whining. She's been doing it ever since the police officer nudged her through my front gate and into my yard.

'She didn't have any family left and the pound's full,' the officer said. 'You'd be doing us a favour if you looked after her dog for a bit.'

Her dog. I hadn't even liked the woman and now I was babysitting the only loved one she'd had left.

I nudge a bowl of dog food a little closer. 'You need to eat.' Josephine just looks at me with those sad Frenchie eyes.

'Yeah, I don't blame you.' The food was straight out of a can the police had found next door. It looks like shit and smells worse. I open the screen door.

'Come inside then.'

She ducks through my legs and heads straight for the fireplace to make herself comfy on the Turkish rug that used to be my mum's. By the time I've locked up for the night, she's asleep.

I watch Josephine chasing lizards in my tiny backyard while I fry off the minced kangaroo meat I found in the back of the freezer. It's been there since Bruno died and the smell brings on a fresh wave of grief. Half a cup each of rice, carrots, zucchini and corn. Then enough water to cook the rice.

Josephine comes when I whistle. 'Give that a go.'

She sniffs the bowl.

'That's what real food tastes like,' I tell her when she's licked it clean. 'I spose you want a walk now, eh? It'll have to wait until the washing's done.'

Wednesday's laundry day. Rain, hail or shine.

My guts are cramping as I hang the washing. Lucky there isn't much these days.

Still, I have to run for the dunny after.

I find Bruno's old lead and we go out through the front gate, but Josephine balks when I turn towards Cranston Street. A strip of blue and white police tape still hangs from the street sign.

'Fair enough.'

I usually avoid the other end of my street because it joins a busy road, but I let Josephine have her way and try to ignore the morning traffic. Up ahead, three women with babies in prams and toddlers in tow are headed our way.

'Come on, time to go home.' But the Frenchie pulls her lead, and I shuffle-run to keep up. We meet the mothers' group and Josephine's the centre of attention. Mums and kids scratch her ears and stroke her back.

'What's her name?' The little boy has deep brown eyes ringed in thick lashes. Just like my son when he was a baby.

I clear my throat. 'Josephine. Her name's Josephine.'

A chorus of 'Josie! Josie!' follows until the mums usher them on.

It takes a minute to get going again. Down a side street away from the main road, there's a dog park, with a high fence and no shade. But it's empty, which is a win.

Josephine takes off at a run as soon as she's through the gate, as if she knows her way around. Was this where my neighbour was headed yesterday? A regular outing turned into a regular tragedy.

See, what did I tell ya?

My guts are cramping again, and the sun scorches my head out of a clear sky.

You wouldn't believe it was cold enough for frost yesterday. I take off my jacket. 'Bloody council.' Why build a dog park without shade or somewhere to sit?

Josephine comes to lean against my leg. Her weight and the regular bellow of her pumping lungs are the most comforting thing I've felt since my wife died.

'I don't know why everyone's getting so worked up,' she'd said when the Prime Minister shut the borders. Laugh was on her, I suppose.

I scrabble in my pocket for a hankie and settle for a crumpled tissue. When I finish wiping my eyes a young woman with short blonde hair lets herself in through the gate behind me, a black and white cavoodle on her heels. It promptly takes a shit.

'Gigi!' The blonde glances at me. She's got a heart-shaped birthmark beside her right eye. 'Sorry, she does it every time.' She tugs a doggy-do bag from the blue dispenser on the fence and makes a face as she scrapes up the mess.

'It stinks.'

She manages to look both embarrassed and cross that I hadn't politely ignored the whole thing. 'Yeah, it usually does.'

Josephine and the cavoodle are busy sniffing each other's bums. 'Not if they're eating the right food.'

'I only buy the expensive stuff.' She tosses the bag in the bin and squirts sanitiser on her hands.

'Doesn't matter how much you pay for it. If it comes out of a can, it's no good.'

'Right. Um, I better go after Gigi.'

She takes off after the cavoodle who's running circles around Josephine in a game that neither is winning.

Plastic takeaway containers are on special so I get a pack of twenty. Thursdays are good for specials, which is why it's shopping day. Rain, hail or shine.

I make up another batch of kangaroo rice plus a chicken meatloaf with hard- boiled eggs from my chickens.

'Try this,' I say to the blonde that afternoon.

She eyes the plastic containers. 'Uh, thanks, but I'm vegetarian.'

I take off the lids and set the containers down. 'It's for the dog.' I whistle and Josephine and Gigi come running. A chihuahua with a scruffy brown coat trots at their heels.

The Frenchie and the chihuahua get stuck into the rice, while Gigi sniffs at the meatloaf.

'She's pretty fussy,' the woman says, but Gigi snatches a slice of the meatloaf with its egg centre and wolfs it down in two big bites. 'Whoa.'

'Better than that tinned rubbish.' She looks a bit miffed.

'Lion! Get out of it!' A redheaded fella grabs the chihuahua by his collar and tugs him away. 'Sorry mate, I wasn't watching.'

'He can have it.'

'What do you use for meat?'

'Kangaroo. It's lean and cheap.'

Josephine laps up the last grains and then comes to lean against my leg. I scratch her behind the ears.

'Brilliant idea. First time here? I haven't seen you before.'

'He was here yesterday too,' the blonde pipes in. 'I think I've seen your dog before though. Does your wife normally bring her?'

My chest squeezes tight around my heart. 'Not my wife, my neighbour. She's dead.'

'Oh shit. I'm so sorry.'

'Don't be, I didn't like her.'

Josephine doesn't like the vacuum, so I sweep out the house with the broom instead, cursing the burn in my shoulders. She follows me as I move through the house, cleaning windows, dusting the cobwebs from the cornices, mopping the kitchen floor. She turns up her nose at the lemon-scented Jiff when I scrub the toilet and takes herself back to her spot between my chair and the fire.

It's slow going. My guts hurt and I feel weaker than a bruised reed.

Fridays used to be bingo at the senior's centre, but it's not the same going on my own. So now Fridays are for housework. Rain, hail or shine.

When I finish, Josephine's snoring. It's as good an excuse as any to push my chair back and have a snooze too.

It's late afternoon before we make it to the dog park. Gigi greets Josephine like an old friend, and they take off to run laps along the fence.

The blonde walks over. 'I'm glad you came today. I didn't see you this morning.'

'Friday's housework day.'

'Sure. I just wanted to say thanks for the food. For Gigi. She's like a whole new dog!'

I look at my feet. 'Dogs need to eat right too.'

'Yeah. My name's Caitlyn by the way.'

'Reggie.'

'Is that short for Reginald? Cool. That's my granddad's name.'

She's bouncing up and down on her toes, like my son used to. He was wired like that, always too much energy to burn.

Might have been what got him into drugs.

My wife's spring daffodils sense a change in the weather. I can see Josephine snuffling their green shoots behind the house while I stir a big pot of stew on the stove. Sweat tickles my hairline and upper lip. It's too hot to be in the kitchen, but Saturday's cook-up day. Rain, hail or shine.

Divvy the stew up into containers and pop them in the freezer. It used to be that a pot of stew barely made a meal in this house, now I have enough for a week. Once the stew's done, I make a chicken meatloaf for Gigi and some kangaroo rice for Lion.

Josephine snatches what doesn't fit in the containers. 'Cheeky bugger.'

She looks up at me when she's done. Her stupid Frenchie grin makes me smile.

The park's full when we get there and a kelpie with a nicked ear tries to hump my leg as I come through the gate.

'Bugger off.'

The kelpie tears off to harass someone else. Josephine follows behind him, slower with her shorter legs.

Lion appears out of the crowd and comes to sniff the plastic bag I'm carrying. I give him a scratch at the base of his tail, just where he likes it.

'He can smell that rice of yours from the next block.' It's the red-haired one, Andrew.

I hand one of the containers over.

'Thanks, mate. Are you sure we can't give you something for it?'

I watch Josephine tackle a mixed breed twice her size. 'Not running a business, am I?'

'You could, you know. People like to spoil their dogs.'

'Yeah, I've noticed,' I say as a Jack Russell pelts past, wearing a pair of bright pink denim overalls.

Caitlyn waves and she and Gigi come to join us. I fish the meatloaf out of the bag and give it to her.

'You're amazing, thanks, Reg!' Her lips leave a warm spot on my cheek. 'I've got something for you too.' She unzips her bag and pulls out a pack of Walker's chewy toffee.

'Where'd you find that?'

'The chemist near my mum's place sells it. I remember you saying it was your favourite.'

I clear my throat, but the words still come out gruff, 'didn't need to buy it just for me.' But she's not listening anyway.

'Hi, I'm Caitlyn. You're Paul's partner, right?' 'He's my husband now, but yeah, I'm Andrew.'

I look from one to the other. 'I thought you lot knew each other.' They laugh.

'Mate, I didn't know anyone in here until I met you. And I've been bringing Lion for nearly two years!'

'It's a bit of a game really, to see how long you can avoid eye contact with the other owners,' says Caitlyn.

'Seems stupid.'

Andrew claps me on the shoulder. 'Yeah, mate, it is.'

Sunday. Day of rest.

I'm stitching a button back on my good shirt and keep stabbing myself with the needle. My eyes are blurry today, my head heavy. Josephine nudges my arm with a cool wet nose, and I set the shirt down to give her a scratch.

'Last one, Frenchie, then we'll go.' Monday's mending day. Rain, hail or shine.

I have to stop twice for a breather on our way to the park. My legs tremble and I wonder if I should have brought my mum's old walking stick. Embarrassing, but at least I wouldn't look like an idiot by falling over.

There's a sharp ache in my guts as I open the gate and let Josephine in. I follow, clinging to the fence line.

Josephine finds Lion and the pair get into a play fight while a black labrador whose coat's going grey watches on from the sidelines. His owner's talking to Andrew and Paul. She must be close to my age but still 'a looker' as my brother used to say.

Andrew, Paul and the older lady join me.

'The black lab's mine,' she says by way of greeting. 'His name's Quincy. I'm Lin.'

'Reggie. The Frenchie's Josephine.'

My voice comes to me from down a tunnel. I look around. 'How hard would it be for them to put in a bloody bench?'

'You right mate?' Andrew puts a hand on my shoulder and I sway into him. Dark spots cluster at the corner of my vision. Paul puts his fingers on my neck. Is he feeling for a pulse?'

'Still kicking, aren't I?'

'I've got a camp chair in my car.' Lin takes off at a run. I bet she doesn't need the Garden Kneeler.

Once they have me in the chair, Paul hunkers down and offers me a bottle of water. I shake my head and put my hand on Josephine when she comes to lean against me.

'Drink.'

'He's a GP,' Andrew says. 'No point in arguing.'

I drink.

Caitlyn drives one of the smallest cars I've ever seen. She opens the back door for Josephine while I lower myself into the passenger seat. My knees touch the glovebox.

'Could've taken the bus.'

'Don't be stupid. What if it was running late and you missed your appointment?' She slips in behind the wheel in one fluid move. 'Where's your list?'

I hand it over. 'The specials—'

'Are better on Thursdays. I know.'

We make good time, and she finds a park right outside the oncology centre.

Thank Christ. Her taste in music is bloody awful. 'I'll be back at two to pick you up.'

I open the door and start levering myself out of the car. She leans over and touches my arm. Squeezes it.

'Good luck.'

I sleep in the next day. Josephine jumps into bed and nudges me with her nose. I wake up long enough to scratch her ears before I slide back into sleep.

Someone's knocking at my door. When I don't answer they knock again.

Josephine's jumping around, barking her snuffling bark.

'Righto, I'm coming.' My body's weighted down with lead chain, but I make it to the door. When I open it, Lion skitters inside, his nails clicking on the floorboards. He rounds up the Frenchie and then they both race back outside through Andrew's legs.

'I'll take her down to the park for a bit and have her back in a few hours.'

I vomit on his shoes. He stares at the mess for a minute and then steers me back to bed.

Paul the GP is chopping carrots in my kitchen. He's got good knife skills. 'Do you cook off the veggies before you add the kangaroo?'

'Yeah, but not too much. Dogs need a bit of bite.'

Josephine and Lion are playing in the backyard. I can hear the chihuahua yipping and the occasional flustered clucking of the chooks.

Paul serves up the risotto into containers and then starts to clean up. 'No need for that. I can do it later.'

'And I can do it now. Just finish your cuppa and try to eat that sandwich, even if you don't feel like it.'

I don't feel like it. But I eat it anyway.

He doesn't look at me when he asks, 'What did your specialist say?'

I swallow a mouthful of bread and ham that tastes like cardboard. 'It's in my lungs now. And my liver.'

Caitlyn drops me home and there's the black lab, Quincy, asleep on my doorstep. I can hear a lawnmower in the backyard.

'Oopsy daisy,' says Lin when she spots me. 'I thought I'd have it done before you got home.' She's all sweaty and red-faced, her dark hair all tucked up inside a wide- brimmed hat. 'Give me a minute, would you, love.'

I get her a glass of water and wait. Josephine comes to sit beside me. Her head's tipped to one side, watching. Maybe she's wondering why this woman I'd only met once was mowing my lawn.

Me and her both.

It's one of my good days but the walk to the dog park still leaves me shaking and lightheaded. Josephine seems to sense it. No tugging on her lead today.

The park's empty. Maybe because of the storm front that's edging over the eastern horizon, pushing a wet breeze ahead of it. There'll be rain soon.

'Go on, bugger off,' I tell the Frenchie, but she doesn't leave my side. 'What's up with you? Go on, get.' She stalks off to sniff at a damp patch next to the fence.

I lean up against the fence myself and try not to fall over. We don't make it home before the rain hits.

The specialist isn't happy. Well, that makes two of us.

'You're lucky someone found you when they did. Pneumonia's going to make things complicated.' She sighs. 'We're going to have to talk about palliative care, Reggie.'

Josephine's warm in my lap. Her snuffling breath is a familiar comfort. I've missed her these last few weeks.

'God, they don't make these things for off-roading, do they?' Andrew pushes my chair in through the gates of the park. The dogs are playing, their owners standing in a row in the middle. They're all smiling, although Lin seems to be crying too.

'What's this then?' They move aside.

There's a bench, made of wood. A sapling planted beside it. A brass plate on the seat back has an inscription that blurs when I read it.

For those who turn up every day. Rain, hail or shine.

Thank you to the Friends of Mansfield Library

The Friends of Mansfield Library Inc (FOML) have sponsored the inaugural Mansfield Readers and Writers Festival with funds to support the publication of this anthology.

Since 1991, the FOMLs have promoted, supported and advocated for the Mansfield Library. They believe in the importance of libraries as community hubs and places of ideas.

How the FOMLs raise funds for Mansfield Library

The FOML fund-raising efforts include running a preloved book shop (the Little Shop of Good Reads) and holding used book sales every two to three months.

They have also applied successfully for a community grant with Community Bank Mansfield & District.

How the FOMLs use the funds they raise

Thanks to the support of Community Bank Mansfield & District, the

FOMLs will provide a self-serve book check out kiosk, to be incorporated into the Mansfield Library as part of the Library refurbishment due for completion in early 2023.

Funds raised by the FOMLs are used for activities that contribute to or align with the Library's programs.

In the last twelve months, the FOMLs have hosted an author visit, run a Mad Hatters' Tea party during Seniors Festival, and contributed to Library activities such as the children's Christmas Party. They have also contributed for several years to the Maternal and Child Health Baby Book Bags. The FOMLs also advocate on issues related to our Library.

How to get involved

The FOMLS always welcome new members to help fund raise and organise events in support of the Library's programs. You can reach the FOMLs and the Little Shop of Good Reads on Facebook or contact them through Mansfield Library.

www.ingramcontent.com/pod-product-compliance
Lightning Source LLC
Chambersburg PA
CBHW020009140726
47904CB00018B/2134